RECLAIMING THE WOLF

Jessie Donovan

Reclaiming the Wolf
Copyright © 2014 Laura Hoak-Kagey
Mythical Lake Press
First Edition

Cover Art by Clarissa Yeo of Yocla Designs.

ISBN 13: 978-1942211082

To the Wolf Pack
Thank you for your support!

Other Books by Jessie Donovan

Asylums for Magical Threats
Blaze of Secrets
Frozen Desires
Shadow of Temptation

Stonefire Dragons
Sacrificed to the Dragon: Parts 1-4
Seducing the Dragon (forthcoming)

Cascade Shifters
Convincing the Cougar
Reclaiming the Wolf
Cougar's First Christmas
Resisting the Cougar (Early 2015)

CHAPTER ONE

Cascade Mountains, Eleven Years Ago

Kaya Alexie kept crouched low behind the thick underbrush of the forest, careful to keep still in her human form, making no more noise than what it took to breathe. If the male cougar-shifter found her before she reached the target, she would lose, and she needed to win if she wanted to claim her prize. Only then could she get what she'd wished for these past few months.

She strained her ears for the slightest sound that might give away the male's hiding spot, but even though her hearing wasn't as good as in her wolf form, all she could hear was the rustling of the leaves and branches and the small scurrying of the ground mice. Apart from the occasional bird cry, nothing seemed out of the ordinary.

Maybe, just maybe, she had finally lost him.

Not that she would be celebrating anytime soon. She'd been secretly dating Sylas Murray, the cougar-shifter from a neighboring clan, for the last six months and she was well aware of how skilled he could be. His tracking skills were damn good, and definitely her biggest obstacle to winning.

Still, she wasn't too bad herself. She could outsmart the other eighteen-year-old wolf-shifters in her pack when it came to tracking and evading drills; it was only a matter of time before she could beat Sylas too.

Maybe even today.

A bird chirped and then flew right past her. She looked up into the trees, but since the sun had set half an hour ago, it was too dark to make out any recognizable shapes. If Sy had made his way into the branches up above, the sneaky cat would use his feline grace to pounce on her. She needed to move.

She itched to shift into a wolf and feel the wind against her fur, but they'd agreed to stay human to make the challenge more difficult. Of course, moving her nearly six-foot tall body through the underbrush without making a sound was no easy feat. Autumn was nearly here, which meant the thick foliage of the understory had turned into a maze of sharp sticks.

She finally broke through the last of the trees at the edge of the clearing and felt a sense of giddiness. Victory was nearly hers for the taking. If she could just make it to the big rock outcropping on the far side, she would win, and Sy would have to give her anything she wanted. That was their deal.

And she knew exactly what she wanted to ask for.

She was tired of looking over her shoulder or finding a way to sneak past her clan's guards and sentries to spend a few stolen hours with her boyfriend. She wanted to show off Sy to the world, and if she won tonight, she was going to invite him to her clan's autumn celebration next week.

Sy accompanying her to the celebration and facing the scrutiny of her entire clan was a big step. Interspecies pairings were still considered taboo among most shifter clans, Kaya's included. Yet, if Sy felt as she thought he felt about her, he wouldn't care about her clan's objections and old-fashioned bullshit. He would stand with her against anything.

But she was getting ahead of herself. First, she needed to make it across the wide-open clearing and be the first to touch the rock.

Kaya sprinted as fast as her long legs would carry her. She had ten feet to go when she heard a cougar growl behind her.

This was the border between her clan and his, and her heart skipped a beat as a million questions and worries raced through her head. Had someone from Sy's clan discovered them? What would Sy do if they had?

Stop being a chicken shit, and see who's following you. She took a deep breath and looked over her shoulder, only to find a naked Sy chasing after her. She stumbled at the sight of his broad chest and strong, lean muscles, but Kaya quickly regained her wits. They had both started this game dressed in clothes and his nakedness could only mean one thing: Sylas Murray was a cheating bastard who had shifted into his cougar form back in the forest.

Despite months of these little games, he'd never cheated before. His shift and disregard for their "human only" rule signaled that he was afraid she could finally beat him.

Her inner wolf growled at his deceit and her human-half agreed with that sentiment.

Well, fuck him. I'm still going to win. She pushed her body harder. It was just a few more feet to the rock, and now more than ever, she was determined to beat her man.

~~~

Sylas Murray noticed Kaya's glare and realized he might actually lose. The woman was beyond determined to beat him.

Normally, he loved the way she challenged him and tried to outsmart him. She being a wolf-shifter and seeing the world differently because of the wolf inside of her was part of the reason he loved her.

From raising her chin in defiance to her grand plans on how to improve relations between shifters and humans, he loved all of it. On top of that, just a hint of her scent drove both him and his inner cougar crazy. His body was always on fire for her, to the point he spent most of his time with a hard cock and a blood-deprived brain.

That was why he needed to win tonight because if he did, he could finally claim Kaya as his own. He was pretty confident Kaya would say yes to his request and allow him to finally make love to her.

As Kaya picked up her pace and raced across the clearing toward the victory rock, Sy drew on the last of his strength to run as fast as he could before he jumped and just barely caught her waist with his hands. As they tumbled to the ground, Sy was careful to take most of the impact. She might be tough, but the thought of her getting hurt because of him made his inner cat snarl.

Once they stopped tumbling and he managed to get Kaya pinned face-down on the ground, he leaned down and nuzzled her neck. He took a deep inhale of her womanly scent, and his already hard cock turned to stone.

Since he wasn't able to pound into Kaya's wet heat just yet, he settled for nipping her earlobe. When she didn't make the little noises of pleasure like usual, he knew she was angry. He wished he could shift into his cougar form and purr to calm her down, a trick he'd learned early on, but she would bolt the second he released her.

He nuzzled her neck again and gently kissed the place where her neck met her shoulder before he said, "Losing isn't the end of the world, Kaya-love. You nearly beat me this time."

Her body went tense below him. She turned her head and narrowed her warm dark chocolate eyes. "I would've beaten you if you hadn't cheated, Sylas Murray." Her voice went low. "Now, let me go."

He wasn't afraid of her cool, simmering anger; he was used to her notorious temper. He simply laced his fingers through hers and squeezed. She tried to tug her hand loose, but with him on top of her, she didn't have enough range to accomplish it. "Cede defeat, and I'll let you up."

She growled. "Why should I? You're the one who cheated. By all accounts, you should cede."

He decided truth was his best option. He gently bit her ear and whispered, "I wanted you too badly to play by the rules. Will you cede, Kaya-love? All I want is you naked and willing beneath me."

Kaya remained motionless under him, but he could smell her arousal. *She wants me, too.*

But he had hurt the woman's pride, and he needed to ease it a little before she would acknowledge her desire.

He'd planned to tell her tonight anyway, but if he told her he loved her, she just might let him off the hook. While he'd said the words a thousand times in his head, he'd been afraid to say them out loud.

Of course, some people, such as his twin brother Kian, would say telling a woman you loved her when she was angry and face down in the dirt might not be the best strategy. But nothing between him and Kaya had ever followed the rules. His gut said it was time.

He lifted his head and looked his wolf-shifter in the eyes as he said, "Please, Kaya. I want to show you how much you mean to me. I love you."

~~~

Kaya's anger eased a little as she heard the words she'd yearned to hear for weeks, if not months, and a plan started to form in her head. There was a chance they might both get what they wanted.

Still, she wasn't about to let her cougar off easy. If she said it was okay to cheat now, the male would do it again. She was going to make him work for it this time. "I don't know if I should believe you. For all I know, you're just trying to get into my pants."

He moved one of his hands from her back to her cheek. As his fingers stroked her skin, it became harder and harder to stay mad at him.

Damn the man and his warm, rough hands.

The corner of his mouth ticked up and Kaya resisted a groan. He knew she was softening.

When he spoke, she nearly shivered at his deep and scratchy voice. "Of course I want to get into your pants. You're my clever, sexy-as-hell girlfriend. I would think you'd be suspicious if I didn't want to."

She tried to shake off his hand so she could think properly, but Sy moved his hand under her hair to the back of her neck and started to caress her skin. One stroke, then another. Each movement sent a thrill through her body that ended between her legs.

What was she castigating him for? Oh, that's right, for cheating.

Somehow, she made her mouth work and said, "Flattery still hasn't made me forget how you cheated. If you cheat at this, then what else won't you cheat at?"

He stopped stroking the skin of her neck as he leaned his forehead against hers. His green eyes were intense, as if they could see straight into her heart. He said, "I would never cheat on you with another female, Kaya. Ever."

The intensity of his words, combined with the emotion in his eyes, caused her to stop breathing for a second. She couldn't help but believe him.

However, she wanted, no needed, more. "Will you always keep your promises to me?"

He squeezed the back of her neck. "From now on, I'll try my hardest. Sometimes things happen that I can't control, but if it's within my power, then yes, Kaya-love, I'll always do what I say from now on."

"Then I'll forgive you on one condition."

He grinned. "Just one? That's very unlike you."

She wriggled and tried to get free, but all it did was remind her that a very naked and aroused man was lying on top of her. While she loved the weight and heat of him, she wanted to face him. "I'm serious. Now, are you going to let me up so we can hash out the details without me lying face down in the grass?"

His grin widened. "I kind of like you under me."

She rolled her eyes. "I know you're only nineteen and teenage boys spend ninety-nine percent of their time thinking about sex, but I need you to focus a little longer."

He squeezed the back of her neck again. "So you're going to let me into your pants?" She gave him a look and he said, "Okay, okay."

Before she could do more than blink, Sy had stood and lifted her up to face him. She slowly brushed the pieces of grass off her top. When Sy made a male noise to hurry up, she bit back a smile. Toying with him was fun.

She spent more time than was necessary brushing off the debris on her breasts and she was rewarded with a growl. She decided that Sy had had enough. Lowering her hands, she looked back up at him.

His gaze was heated and she resisted the urge to jump him just yet. Instead, she said, "Can you focus long enough to listen to my condition?"

"What's your condition?"

She closed the distance between them and ran her hand up his naked chest, loving the way her palm felt against his dark spattering of hair, and rested it on the back of his neck. He shifted his body a little, and she was suddenly aware of his very hard cock between them.

Focus, Kaya. You might still be a virgin, but it's not like you haven't seen him naked before. "I want you to be my date for GreyFire's autumn celebration."

For a second, he said nothing and she started to wonder if she'd asked him too soon. Then he raised an eyebrow and said, "Are you sure?"

She let out the breath she'd been holding. "Yes. You love me, and despite your enormous ego, I love you too. I think it's time to stand up to our clans and fight for it."

His gaze was heavy-lidded and his voice was husky when he said, "Say it again."

"What? That you have an enormous ego?"

He grabbed her ass and pulled her flush up against him. His eyes were almost dangerous. "No, the part about how you love me."

The pressure of his hard, hot cock against her belly was making it difficult to think of anything, but she managed to say, "I love you, Sylas Murray. Will you go on a non-secret date with me?"

He leaned his face down and kissed the right corner of her mouth. "Yes." Then he kissed the left corner. "Anything for you, Kaya-love."

She moved her hips against him, and he drew in a breath. She smiled, drunk on the power she had over him. "Then hurry up and get me naked, Sy, so you can make love to me."

~~~

Sy was still trying to absorb how Kaya wanted to present him to her clan, but then the little vixen rubbed against his dick, and all other thoughts went out the window.

Tonight, he was finally going to make love to the stubborn woman who'd stolen his heart.

He gave her a quick, rough kiss before grabbing the hem of her shirt, and she lifted her arms so he could tug it over her head.

15

Tossing it to the side, he rubbed his hands up and down her bare arms before reaching around her back for the hooks of her bra.

The damn thing didn't want to go free and he nearly sliced it with a claw, but he rather liked the lacy blue bra against her bronze skin and would like to see Kaya in it later. So he fumbled with the hooks and finally released them. He then rubbed the skin between her shoulder blades, loving how soft her skin was there.

By all rights, he should take his time, maybe even use the material of her bra to tease her nipples, but Sy was impatient. A teenage boy could only hold back for so long. All he could think about was feeling her tight, wet heat around his cock.

Tossing the bra aside, he was distracted by her dark, hard nipples.

He'd spent many a night dreaming about them in his mouth. He couldn't resist tracing one, and then the other with his finger before he bent down and took her right nipple into his mouth. He sucked her deep before gently biting her sensitive skin. Kaya moaned and arched her back into his touch. He gave one last pull, and then released her to look his wolf-shifter in the eye. As much as it was killing him to hold back, he said, "We've always stopped here before. Are you sure about going the rest of the way, Kaya? I love you, and will wait as long as it takes."

His heart kicked into overdrive as she brushed her hand over his chest, her fingers playing with his hair there. Her touch was like a brand with heat flaring from her soft fingertips.

Then she started to move her hand lower and he went still. He hadn't lied; he could wait. But he hoped like hell her hand would keep going.

And it did. She traced the line of hair toward his groin, but stopped shy of touching the head of his cock currently curled up against his belly. She'd seen it before, even touched it, but then she did something she hadn't done before and traced the tip with her finger.

His legs wanted to buckle, but he somehow found a way to remain standing. She traced his slit once, and then again. As he let out a drop of precum, he knew he wasn't going to last as long as he wanted the first time.

He watched as Kaya touched the bead of wetness on his cock, raised her finger to her mouth, and sucked it deep. He nearly came right then and there. In a strangled voice he said, "Kaya, you're killing me."

She removed her finger from her mouth and smiled. "Does that answer your question?"

Holy fuck, how he deserved this vixen, he didn't know, but he needed to kiss her. Now.

~~~

Kaya didn't really know what the hell she was doing. She'd never tried to seduce a man before, but Sy seemed to like it. As she tasted the saltiness of Sy's precum, she decided she would try more of that later. Right now, with Sy's eyes blazing down at hers, she barely had time to draw a breath before his lips were on hers.

His tongue thrust into her mouth as he pulled her up against him. She moaned as her nipples pressed against his hot chest, but she wanted to feel even closer to him. She ran a hand into his hair and battled his tongue for control, their teeth clashing in the challenge.

Wrapping his arms around her, he surrounded her in his heat and the musky male scent that was Sy. Wetness rushed between her legs and her core started to pulse. She tried rubbing her clit against his leg, but instead of helping her, Sy broke the kiss and said, "I think it's time to get you naked."

Without a word, she undid her pants and kicked them off before shedding her underwear. A moment of embarrassment came over her as Sy gave her a long look from head to breast to the hair between her legs. Men had seen her naked after a shift, but this was different. It felt like Sy was caressing her body with his eyes.

He placed a finger under her chin and raised her face until she met his eyes. Her breath caught. His gaze was hot, his eyes like liquid green gold, and it made her feel as if she were the most desirable woman in the world.

He moved his finger from her chin to her lips. As he traced the bottom one with his warm, rough finger, he said, "You have nothing to be embarrassed about. You're the most beautiful woman in the world to me. I could stare at your naked body for hours, and still not get my fill."

"Oh, Sy." She touched his hand on her cheek. "I love you."

"If you love me now, let's see what you say after I'm done."

She opened her mouth to make a quip, but before she could say anything, he scooped her up and laid her on the ground. As he covered her body with the weight of his very hard, very masculine body, Kaya, the six-foot tall wolf-shifter, actually felt delicate.

He gave her a quick kiss before he leaned up and ran his hands down her neck, cupped her breasts, and then ran his hands over the muscled planes of her stomach. "You're perfect to me, and always will be, Kaya-love."

Reclaiming the Wolf

She felt her cheeks flush. As he continued his journey down to her core, she lost the power of speech. After six months, this was really happening. Kaya was about to lose her virginity to a cougar-shifter.

~ ~ ~

Sy had been going slow for Kaya's benefit, but now, as he reached the folds between her legs, he couldn't believe he was finally going to feel the tight, wet heat of her pussy.

He traced one swollen lip, and then the other. At a breathy, "Sy," he looked up. Kaya's dark brown eyes were heavy-lidded, and while there was a touch of color on her tan cheeks from embarrassment, he could see she wanted what he was promising.

He pushed his finger inside her tight, slick heat. She gasped, and Sy said, "Last chance, Kaya-love. Say the word, and I'll stop."

Kaya started to move on his finger, and if he hadn't already fallen in love with her, he would've in that instant.

He gave one deep thrust before removing his finger. Licking her wetness off his skin, he looked Kaya dead in the eye and said, "You won't regret it, love. I promise."

She wriggled. "Please, Sy. I'm more than ready for you to be my first."

Spreading her legs wide, he rubbed his hands up and down the smooth skin of her inner thighs. Her heart was beating so fast he could feel her pulse where her thigh met her hip.

Her heart wasn't the only one beating a million times a minute. The smell of her arousal, combined with the warm feel of her skin against his palms, pushed his need to claim her to the bursting point. He would force himself to take this slowly if it killed him, which it very well might, but he couldn't resist claiming her with words.

He squeezed her thighs and growled low before he whispered, "If I have anything to say about it, I will be your first and your last."

Her eyes widened, but his gaze moved to focus on the wet, swollen flesh between her thighs. He'd waited months to brand the taste of her sweet honey on his memory, and his mouth watered in anticipation.

He leaned down and licked her from slit to clit, causing her to cry out. Fuck, her taste was incredible. He licked her hot sweetness again, and again, but it wasn't enough.

As he started to fuck her sweet pussy with his tongue, he felt Kaya's claws digging into his scalp. This, right here in the clearing, was the best moment of his life. He had a woman he loved, hot and open to him, moaning his name, and who loved him in return. A life together between a cougar-shifter and a wolf-shifter wouldn't be easy, but Kaya was a precious treasure he would do anything to protect.

CHAPTER TWO

Cascade Mountains, Present Day

Kaya Alexie signed her name for the two-hundredth time this morning, tossed aside her pen, and leaned back in her chair. Until she'd become GreyFire's clan leader three years ago, she'd never known just how much paperwork was involved. But if she didn't fill out the monthly shifter report for the US Bureau of Shifter Affairs, she wouldn't qualify for the grants her researchers desperately needed. She may not like it, but she'd do anything for her clan.

Well, almost anything.

Rather than think about that, Kaya stretched her arms over her head and rotated her shoulders. She finished her stretches just as someone knocked on the door; her next appointment was right on time.

Putting a leg up on her desk, she crossed the other one over it as she said, "Come in."

The door opened to reveal her tall, smiling second-in-command, Erika Washington.

Closing the door, she then made her way to the chairs in front of Kaya's desk, tossed a file on it, and plopped down. "Did you finish the report?" Kaya nodded, and Erika's face turned serious. "Good. Because we have more important things to talk about."

She eyed her friend and commander with suspicion. "If you say 'planning the autumn celebration,' I might just have to throw my shoe at you."

Erika grinned, her white teeth blazing in contrast to her dark skin. "Oh, come on. It's one of the few times you actually let down your hair and wear a dress. I'm sure all of the males are counting down the days."

Kaya rolled her eyes. "I knew you had a second agenda. We've discussed this before, Erika. I'm fine without a mate. Slapping a ring on some random male isn't going to automatically make me a better leader."

Erika shook her head. "That's not entirely true. The wolf part of us needs the stability of our leader having a mate. You've done wonders bringing our clan back from the near-bankruptcy caused by your uncle, but it's time to at least try finding a male worthy of having at your side, and not just for our sakes, but for yours too."

"I've managed fine so far, and it's not like you can just force things to happen just because you want them to. I envy leaders like Kian Murray, who has a mate he can lean on, but it's harder for female leaders. You know what shifter males are like. Too many of them want to dominate and take over, and the hell if I'll let that happen."

Erika put her hands on Kaya's desk and leaned forward, causing the small braids of her hair to swing around her shoulders. "I'm not asking you to step into an arranged marriage. I'm just asking for you to socialize at the autumn celebration." Kaya opened her mouth, but Erika cut her off. "Not just talking with people, but actually accept offers when males ask you to dance."

"Hmph. And to think, I thought I was the one in charge here."

"Kaya, I'm serious. It's time to forget about Sylas Murray and find a nice wolf-shifter to mate with."

It'd been years since anyone had mentioned that name to her, and for good reason. "I stopped caring about that damn cat the day he broke my heart."

Erika raised her eyebrows. "Liar."

Kaya sighed. "Will dancing with some males get you off my back?"

Her friend smiled. "Part of my job is to look after you. Good thing, too, or you'd never stop working."

Work was what had helped her focus and find her place in the clan, but she didn't want to have that discussion with Erika. Instead, Kaya smiled at her friend and said, "Fine, I'll do some dancing. But don't start making plans for any mating or pup celebrations just yet."

Erika clapped her hands. "Good." She waved a hand toward the file she'd placed on the desk earlier, and leaned back into her chair again. "Now that's settled, I need to talk to you about the bids for our latest malaria drug. The discrimination against drugs developed using bits of shifter DNA is starting to lessen. If the FDA approves it next year, this drug might be the key to our clan's financial stability."

Luckily, Kaya was used to Erika's whipping from one topic to another, and didn't bat an eye at the sudden change of topic. She picked up the file her friend had brought, opened it, and said, "Okay, walk me through the proposed bids."

Erika had just started to go over the expected profit margins when the phone on her desk started ringing. She glanced down at the screen and saw the name of one of her most experienced sentries currently on duty. Since he wouldn't call unless something important had happened, Kaya picked up the receiver and said, "Tell me what's up, Jonathan."

On the other end of the line, Jonathan said, "I found some intruders near Marker 12. All three of them smell like cougars, which is fine, I can handle that. But they have some sort of bag with them and any time I try to inspect it, they growl at me and tell me not to open it."

"There must be something else, or you wouldn't have called me. What aren't you telling me?"

Jonathan's voice became tight. "One of the cougars is Sylas Murray, and he says the bag might contain the beginnings of an epidemic. He wants to talk with you."

Kaya leaned back in her chair. Regardless of whatever she felt about Sy, she knew Kian, the cougar-shifters' clan leader, would only have sent him to GreyFire's land if it was important.

She ignored Erika's quizzical look and took a deep breath before she answered, "Give him the phone."

"I locked him and his two cougar friends inside the sentry shelter. Give me a second."

As she waited for Jonathan to unlock the door and go inside, she steeled herself for the upcoming conversation with Sy. She might be clan leader of the biggest wolf-shifter pack on the west coast, but her stomach churned with nervousness at the thought of talking with the man she'd once loved enough to consider leaving her clan behind for.

Would he be civil? Or kind? Or had the army hardened him and completely changed the teasing, cocky man of her teenage years into a stranger? There was so much she didn't know about him anymore.

But she shouldn't care. She needed to sound strong, cool, and collected. The last thing she wanted was for Sylas Murray to know how much she'd thought of him over the years. At least the conversation was over the phone. It was much easier to keep her voice steady that way.

Erika was frowning at her, but luckily Jonathan's voice came back over the line and she could put up a hand to stall Erika's questions. Jonathan said, "Okay, here's the cougar bastard."

She smiled at his tone. Knowing her clan had her back gave her the necessary courage to remain calm when Sy's voice came on the line. "Kaya?"

She'd always loved the deepness of his voice, but time had added a bit of gravel to it as well. "Yes, it's me. Now tell me why you're trespassing on my land and babbling about some epidemic."

The line was silent a second before Sy replied, "I think you've taken this clan leader thing a little too seriously."

She growled. Apparently, Sy was one of those shifter males who didn't take kindly to a woman being in charge. He never would've said that to his brother or the male leader of the bears.

Well, screw him. She was going to pull out her alphaness and not hold back. "I don't care what you think. Tell me why you're on my land, or I'll have Jonathan call the law enforcement liaisons and they'll cart your ass off to jail."

"Hey, part of the reason I'm here is to try to save all your asses, so you should try being a little nicer to me."

Kaya pinched the bridge of her nose. "Now is not the time to challenge me, Sylas. Unlike the games when we were teenagers,

I can win this one. This is your last chance to tell me why the fuck you're on GreyFire's land."

~~~

Sy wished Kaya was standing in front of him so he could give her his best glare. The woman took things more seriously than his twin brother, which was saying something. Since Kian's recent recovery, his brother had spent most of his days hashing out details with his mate about how to improve the clan's future and stability.

Remembering his brother, Sy took a deep breath and focused on his mission. He'd promised to see this through, and "clan leader mode" Kaya or not, he would do it. "Earlier this week, three mentally unstable wolf-shifters attacked Kian and Trinity. I don't know if they are yours or not, but something was wrong with them. Their eyes glowed purple."

"Purple?"

"We don't know much about wolf-shifter biology, but I'm guessing from your tone this isn't normal."

"Just because I've never heard of it doesn't mean it doesn't exist. What's in the bag you won't let Jonathan investigate?"

He eyed the large black bag being protected by his two clan members. "When Kian was attacked—he's fine, thanks for asking by the way—he killed two of them in self-defense. Our other clan members trapped the remaining wolf, but it refuses to shift back into human form. We need to know what caused their insanity and weird symptoms in case there are more purple-eyed wolves roaming the mountains. To do that, I brought one of the dead wolf-shifters to GreyFire because we need your help."

Each of the shifter clans had focused on specializing in one area, mostly to remain competitive. Until recently, very few shifters had gone to college. The DarkStalker cougar-shifters had become stellar engineers, but lacked sufficient skills in the medical sciences, which GreyFire excelled at. He was confident Kaya would help them, but he had no idea at what price.

Her voice came back on the line. "Let's say I help you. What's in it for GreyFire?"

"If this sickness is contagious, we need to find a way to stop it from spreading. I'm sure an epidemic is the last thing you want."

He could hear something squeak on the other end of the line, as if Kaya were leaning forward in her chair. "Has anyone from your clan showed symptoms? If you've infected Jonathan, or any other of my clan members, by coming here without thinking things through, then consider the truce between our clans over."

He'd threatened the truce once before, almost eleven years ago. "Well, then let's just hope my luck hasn't changed from the last time I nearly broke the truce."

"Nice to hear you view breaking my heart as a lucky escape."

Fuck, he hadn't intended for it to come out that way. He'd been doing so well up until now. "Kaya—"

"No, don't go there. I don't need your apologies or pity. Just tell me if there have been any symptoms inside your clan."

He was dying to ask her why she'd brushed him off without a word all those years ago, but decided getting Kaya to agree to help them was more important right now. "It's been nearly four days since the attack, and no one's shown any symptoms, not even Kian, who was bitten several times by the infected wolves."

"That's all well and good, but what about you and your people? Or even the bag you brought the dead shifter in?"

Sy was starting to understand just how little she viewed his intelligence these days. "I may be many things, but I'm not an idiot. My people and I were tested thoroughly, but nothing showed up. Also, the FierceRiver tigers in India designed the bag we brought with us. Not even the Ebola virus could escape once that thing is sealed up. As an added precaution, the outside of the bag was thoroughly disinfected before we left home."

The FierceRiver tigers rivaled GreyFire's skills in medical science. He knew Kaya would trust the bag to do its job, but would she trust him and his clan? As one of Kian's inner circle of guardians, it was his job to oversee anything his brother couldn't do himself. It was the only reason he'd agreed to step foot on GreyFire's land.

He'd tried to warn his brother about Kaya hating him. He just hoped his brother had been right about how Kaya would take care of her clan and not focus on what had happened between them in the past.

Deep down, however, he was a little disappointed he couldn't be doing this in person. He was curious to see what an older version of Kaya Alexie looked like.

Since she still hadn't answered him, he said, "Well? Are you going to help us or not?"

After another second, she growled into the line, and he nearly smiled. "I had put you on mute to discuss things with my second-in-command. Unlike you, some of us like to think things through first."

She was referring to him leaving her, but he wasn't rising to the bait this time. "So, what did you come up with?"

"You're going to stay there with Jonathan until a biohazard team can retrieve the wolf. Then you're going to leave and wait for my call."

"I'm not going home until I know the results."

"Sy, you staying on my land isn't going to accomplish anything. Go home. I'll call Kian when I have something to report."

There was a reason his brother had made him promise to stay until they knew the results. Their truce with the wolves was tentative at best, and while he wanted to believe Kaya ran things differently, the previous GreyFire leader had kept important information from DarkStalker in the past.

On one occasion, when a group of illegal human poachers had come to the area, that lack of information had ended up taking the life of a mother cougar-shifter and her two cubs.

He quickly assessed the situation and decided there was only one way to ensure he stayed on GreyFire's land. Sy shifted his weight and lowered the phone before spinning around and landing an uppercut to Jonathan's jaw. Thanks to Sy's faster feline reflexes, the wolf didn't have time to brace himself and the punch landed clean. Jonathan fell to the ground unconscious.

His two clan members merely stared at him in curiosity, knowing he only would have punched out the wolf with a good reason. Sy put the phone back to his ear to hear Kaya saying, "Sy? What's going on? Sylas? Are you there?"

He flexed his hand and said, "I just punched out your sentry, so now you're going to have to detain me. I'll be waiting."

With that, he clicked off the phone and went to work on securing the wolf's hands behind him. He couldn't let the sentry escape before he was sure he and his two clan members could stay.

CHAPTER THREE

Two days later, as the last GreyFire researcher left her office, Kaya let out a sigh of relief. Whatever had affected the dead wolf-shifter was no longer contagious, at least as long as no one came into contact with the dead wolf's stool. And since everything related to that wolf-shifter was locked up tight in the infectious diseases research wing, her clan was safe. For now.

Yet there was still the risk of other infected wolves roaming GreyFire's land, especially since they didn't yet know what had caused the wolf's eyes to turn purple or what made them go insane. Her sentries had searched the mountain, but had come up with nothing.

She needed access to both the location where the attack with the sick wolves had taken place and to the rest of DarkStalker's land, but the cougars' leader, Kian, had given her the worst possible answer. He couldn't spare any of his other clan members right now. If she wanted to investigate the place where the attack had happened and/or visit the remaining purple-eyed wolf on his land, she'd have to ask Sy to guide her.

Oh, and she could only bring two people from her clan with her.

She understood Kian's caution considering the relations between her uncle and DarkStalker's former leader. They had not been friendly with one another. However, she was determined to work hard to change the old perceptions and to start building trust between them. That way, if something happened again in the future, both of their clans would be prepared.

In addition, if they were extremely lucky, they might one day get ShadowClaw, the bear-shifter clan in the Cascade Mountains, to trust them both too.

However, her grand schemes would have to wait. For now, she needed to talk with Sylas.

She had put off questioning him as long as possible, but with the immediate threat taken care of,and Sy and his people deemed "clean" of infection, she had no excuse to avoid talking with him. She was clan leader; her past didn't matter. Only the future well-being of her clan was important.

It was time to set things straight.

Leaving her office, she maneuvered the web of corridors carved out of the stone of the mountain, careful to take a path that would steer clear of Erika or any of Kaya's other commanders. It'd taken her time to work up her nerve to talk with her ex, and being sidetracked might make her lose it.

As she moved through the corridors, she ran her hand against the smooth, cool rock that made up most of the walls of her clan's home. GreyFire hadn't always lived in rooms carved out of the mountains. At one time, they'd been forced to eke out an existence in the woods.

But after World War II, each shifter clan had been granted a parcel of land to call home. While their original living spaces had been crude, the advancement of technology now allowed the shifters of the Cascades to power their small subterranean cities inside the mountains via geothermal energy.

Still, as she finally hit the cool air of late-September, the wolf inside of Kaya wanted to howl at finally being outside.

31

All too often, her clan duties kept her cooped up. She itched to shift and go for a run, but that would require shedding her clothes. The last thing she wanted was to be naked when she faced Sy face-to-face for the first time in more than a decade.

All of a sudden, memories of the final time she'd been naked with Sy, while he'd taken her from behind under the full moon, filled her head. His touch had been warm and rough, his caresses loving. Add that to his hard cock pounding into her and filling her to the point of almost pain, and she couldn't remember ever screaming as loud as she had when she'd come back then.

A longing she'd tried to deny, about wanting a male to fuck her because she was a female and not because she was clan leader, rushed forth, but Kaya quickly pushed the feeling aside. Seeing Sy was going to be painful enough; she didn't need a reminder of how he'd wanted her back when she'd been nothing but a slightly naive young woman.

Irritated with herself, she picked up her pace. Why the hell was she thinking about sex with Sy in the first place? The man had promised her the world, only to leave her when her uncle, GreyFire's former clan leader, had applied the slightest amount of pressure.

The asshole hadn't even bothered to say good-bye. He sure as hell didn't deserve her lusty thoughts, no matter how much she'd enjoyed his cock or the feel of his hot, hard body over hers.

Stop it, Kaya. You're not a damn sex-crazed teenager. She walked faster. The sooner she reached the sentry shelter, the sooner she could finally kick Sylas Murray out of her life for good.

~~~

Sy shuffled the deck of cards in his hands, and then looked to Aidan and Danika, the two clan members who'd accompanied him here. "Double or nothing?" he asked.

Aidan pushed his chair back from the table and put up his hands. "I'm done. If I bet any more sentry duty hours, I'll be fifty before I can finish them."

Sy grinned. "You're no fun." He looked to Dani. "Are you up for it, missy?"

Dani narrowed her eyes. "Call me 'missy' again and see what happens."

"I would, but I'd rather stay conscious just in case our host ever decides to make an appearance."

Aidan crossed his arms over his chest. "Remember, she's the leader here, Sy. Irritating her too much might cost the clan."

Sy's grin faded. "I know." He placed the deck of cards in the middle of the table and leaned back in his chair. "But it's been two days. If she doesn't come soon and let us know what her researchers discovered with their tests, I might have to irritate her, if only to get her attention."

Dani shrugged. "She'll have to let us out eventually. I'm sure she doesn't want to make Kian into an enemy, especially since DarkStalker is due to upgrade some of their geothermal turbines over the next year."

Sy stood up. "They could always find someone else to do the upgrade. Everyone keeps talking about our truce, but it hasn't been more than a formality since we were children. That forest fire twenty-five years ago was the only time I remember seeing the wolves and cougars working side by side."

Aidan gave him a long look. "I suspect it'll be different one day. Things have changed dramatically in just the last decade. You even hear of a few humans pairing up with shifters now. I imagine cross-species pairings will happen more often, too."

Sy turned toward Aidan. If his friend was going to touch on his painful past, Sy was going to do the same. "The day you mate a human is the day I'll start to take your words seriously."

Aidan's jaw clenched. "Never."

Dani moved between them and looked from Sy to Aidan and back again. "Really? You two are going to play the game of 'who has the biggest dick' when it comes to shitty pasts?"

Rather than answer, Sy turned away and moved to the window to check for any sign of Kaya. But it was just Jonathan and one other sentry still guarding them.

With no GreyFire leader to distract him, Sy was about to turn back around to apologize to his friend when he saw her. He felt like he'd been punched in the gut.

Kaya was striding toward the house, her walk full of confidence and control. She was older, but no less beautiful. Her long, black hair was pulled back from her face into a messy ponytail-bun crossover, which only highlighted the bronze-tanned planes of her face and the plumpness of her lips. Her long legs were encased in tight jeans, and her form-fitting t-shirt showed off her breasts.

Damn, she was beautiful. Despite everything that had happened, he remembered what it'd been like to lick every inch of her smooth, bronze skin. He'd lapped between her thighs and had never been able to get enough of her taste. He could remember what it felt like to have her beaded nipples rub against his chest as he held her close and fucked her senseless.

Judging by the amount of blood rushing to his cock, it remembered too.

Fuck. He wasn't about to let Kaya see him with a hard-on.

He pictured old, overweight grannies in bikinis and his semi-hard dick started to soften. By the time Kaya was a few feet from the door, his erection was gone. *And you're going to stay that way, buddy.*

He turned and moved to stand next to Aidan and Dani as he said, "Kaya's here."

He kept his gaze trained on the door and willed his face into a mask of cocky indifference. There was no way in hell he was going to let Kaya know how much he was still hurting from her past actions, let alone how he still thought of her as the most beautiful woman he'd ever met.

~~~

Kaya's stomach had been twisting in knots the entire walk to the sentry shelter. As much as she hated it, she was anxious to see the man who'd haunted her dreams for a decade. He'd been an asshole, yes, but he was still the only man she'd ever loved and the best fuck she'd ever had. Her girlish memories refused to let him go.

Because of that, if he looked at her with hatred, or worse, indifference, she wasn't sure how she'd react.

Damn him. She usually had confidence in spades. She was clan leader, for fuck's sake, and that hadn't been an easy thing to accomplish. Yet in this moment, she was as insecure as a fifteen-year-old girl.

The sooner she banished Sy from her life, the better. Hopefully, a one-on-one meeting could finally put all of this mess behind them. Erika had been right about the clan needing their leader to have a mate. She wasn't in a hurry, but she knew deep down that until she stopped comparing every man to Sy's looks, sense of humor, and his ability to please her when naked, she'd never find someone else good enough.

As she reached the shelter and saw her two clan members standing guard, Kaya was reminded of her duty. She was clan leader, and she needed to protect her clan. Screw Sylas Murray. She wanted answers, and he was going to give them to her.

She nodded at Jonathan and said, "Any trouble?"

"Apart from him punching me in the face two days ago, no. They mostly sit around and play cards."

She shrugged. "You'd probably do the same thing if you were cooped up without any internet or TV."

"Yeah, but they're cats. I had expected them to nap all day and play with string."

Kaya laughed and then shook her head. "I'll be sure to suggest that. Now, open the door."

As he unlocked it, Jonathan said, "Do you want us to come in with you?"

"No, but if I need help, I'll call for it."

He nodded and stepped aside. Kaya took a deep breath to calm her stomach, turned the handle, and opened the door.

And there he was, standing on the far side of the room, his two clan members flanking him on either side. While he was still tall with piercing green eyes, pale skin, and dark hair, his shoulders and arms were more muscled than the last time she'd seen him. And his two-day old dark whiskers gave him a rough, grizzled appearance that sent a little thrill through her at the thought of those whiskers rubbing against her inner thighs as he fucked her with his tongue.

Ah, yes. She remembered his tongue.

Reclaiming the Wolf

What the hell am I doing? She pushed the emerging sexual fantasy out of her head, squared her shoulders, and shut the door behind her. In a calm, cool voice she said, "Hello, Sylas."

He raised an eyebrow. "So her highness finally decided to grace us with her presence, huh?"

She resisted taking his bait. "My researchers finished their examinations and determined the wolf isn't contagious as long as it's locked up tight. Also, you three have been cleared of charges. But before I send you home, I want to talk with Sylas. Alone."

Sy stared at her a second and she wondered if she'd have to pull out her attitude card to get him to agree to the demand. But then he said, "Okay."

Leave it to the man to be unclear. "Okay to the meeting, okay to you leaving, or to both?"

"For now, let's say okay to the meeting." He looked from one of his clan members to the other and said, "Dani, Aidan, stay right outside. If she starts ripping out my guts, then I'll call you."

The older DarkStalker male to Sy's right said, "Knowing you, if she starts tearing out your guts, you deserve it."

"Whose side are you on?"

The red-haired DarkStalker female to Sy's left rolled her eyes, leaned around him, and grabbed Aidan's arm. "It's Sy's job to piss her off, not yours. Let's go before you two males fuck up things beyond repair."

Kaya resisted a smile at the DarkStalker female's words.

But as the female passed Kaya on the way to the door, she stopped and fixed her with an intense stare. "You've hurt him enough, and even though he can be an ass, if you cause him any more pain, I'll gouge out your eyes myself, treaty be damned."

While her inner wolf growled at the comment, Kaya didn't blink an eye. She'd encountered much tougher and severe threats in the three years she'd been leader. She merely tilted her head and said, "I'd like to see you try."

The woman growled, but Aidan opened the door and pulled her through. Once the door clicked shut, she was finally alone with Sylas Murray. But as he stared at her with his green eyes, assessing her, she hesitated.

Sure, she was clan leader, but right here, right now, she was just a woman standing in a room with the man who had broken her heart.

~~~

Judging from Kaya's interaction with Dani, the wolf who'd once been strong but naive had morphed into a confident leader who didn't take shit from anyone. An average person might think she was fearless, but he noticed how her thumbs rubbed the pinkies on each of her hands. Kaya always did that when she was nervous.

That thought unsettled him; for some reason, he didn't want her to be nervous around him. A part of his brain suggested pushing her up against the wall and kissing her until she couldn't breathe, and he nearly startled. The woman had broken his heart. Kissing her should be the last thought on his mind.

With a deep breath, he got his shit together and decided he needed to ease the tension in the air so they could get this over with. "It's not like I'm going to shift and attack you or anything, so calm the hell down and tell me what you want."

Her hands balled into fists. Good. He'd rather she be angry. "I see age hasn't brought you manners."

He shrugged. "They come out for special occasions." He took a step toward her. "I'm assuming you already talked to my brother about what you found, so what was so urgent that you needed to talk to me?"

"First, I never said it was urgent, just that I wanted to talk to you alone."

She took a step toward him. She was now close enough that he caught the uniquely feminine scent that was Kaya. It took everything he had to not walk over, lower his head to her neck, and take a deep whiff of woman and grass that was uniquely hers. His cougar didn't care about what had happened between him and the wolf; his cat just wanted to scent-mark her.

Kaya didn't seem to notice his struggle as she continued, "And second, if we're going to work together, I want to lay a few ground rules."

He blinked. "What? Since when are we working together?"

She crossed her arms over her chest and it took every iota of his being not to stare down at her breasts. "You can thank your brother for that one. I need to investigate where the attack took place, and apparently, you're the only one he can spare for the job."

Damn him. This had the scent of Kian's meddling. There were plenty of lower-downs who could show Kaya's people around.

That made him realize something. "Why you? I'd think you'd have more than enough to occupy you here."

"The reasons are my own, and I don't need to share them with you."

Well, then. "Okay, Ms. Leader, can you at least tell me your planned ground rules? That way I can approve or veto them."

Kaya clenched her jaw and moved in front of him. "This, right here with you trying to hold sway over what I do, needs to stop. Yes, you've seen me naked, and yes, we had planned to be

39

mates. But all of that is over, so it's time for you to accept the choices you made and treat this situation with the seriousness it deserves."

Any lustful thoughts he had vanished. He narrowed his eyes. He wasn't about to let her remarks go. "Me? Yes, I fucked up. I was scared of your uncle and I ran, but I tried to make it up to you. Hell, I wrote you a letter nearly every day for a year, but you never replied in all that time, not once."

Kaya blinked. "What?"

He itched to grab her arms and bring her close, but somehow he resisted. "Don't pretend you don't know how your uncle and DarkStalker's old clan leader forced me to join the army to get away from you. I was young, and had fucked up, but I loved you and tried to make it right. You were the one who was childish and couldn't even bother to send a one sentence letter to tell me how your feelings had changed." He leaned his face down to hers. "You're the one who broke my heart, Kaya Alexie, so stop trying to blame me for the shittiness of your decision."

CHAPTER FOUR

Kaya stared at Sy and tried to make her mouth work, but his words just kept repeating inside her head. *I was young, and had fucked up, but I loved you and tried to make it right.*

The way he'd said it, full of anger and a little pain, put a crack in the wall she'd built around herself on the way here to make her feel nothing for Sylas Murray.

Her uncle had never supported Sy as her choice of mate. When she'd brought him to the autumn celebration all those years ago and introduced him as her boyfriend, her Uncle Frances had taken one look at Sy and turned away. The majority of her clan had followed his lead.

But Sy had kept her close to his side the entire evening. He'd even managed to tease a laugh out of her as they danced in the middle of the room with her clan watching, their glares not fazing him one bit. If anything, the stares and looks had made him draw her tighter against him.

To this day, that had been one of the happiest days of her life, and all because of the man now standing less than a foot away from her.

His eyes were hot and angry, burning straight into her, and Kaya decided to put aside her visit to DarkStalker's land for a moment. She needed to know his side of the story, and this might be her only chance to get it. While she'd investigated Sy after he'd left, she'd never come across one of his letters. Even after he had come back from his tours in Iraq, she'd kept her distance, afraid to see him happy with anyone else.

But she needed to know if he was telling the truth, and she couldn't do that without more information.

She held his gaze, took a deep breath, and said, "I never knew about the letters."

He frowned and took a step back. "You're lying."

She shook her head. "No." She stepped toward him and looked up into his eyes. "I. Never. Received them." She should leave it at that, but she burned with curiosity. Before she could change her mind, she forced herself to ask, "What did they say?"

His face went expressionless and she instantly knew he wasn't going to elaborate.

It shouldn't matter what his decade-old letters said, as they were both different people now. Hell, she was in charge of an entire clan. But her inner wolf didn't like the unknowing. Answers would allow the wolf to forget about the cougar and sniff out a new, stronger mate who would look after their pups.

Before Kaya could repeat her question, something flashed in his eyes. But it was gone before she could tell what it was. Then he said, "I didn't come here to talk about our past, and what might've been. In case you've forgotten, there could be crazy wolf-shifters roaming the land, ready to infect your people. I'll work with you because my brother asked me to, but once this is over, I think it's best if we go back to avoiding each other."

She narrowed her eyes at his harsh tone. To think she'd been questioning his assholery. "Of course I'm aware there might be infected shifters roaming the mountains." She poked him in the chest. "My people have spent the last two days combing our territory, but they haven't found anything. That is the only reason

I'm going to step foot on DarkStalker's land. If there's information there, I want to know it." She moved away from the cougar-shifter and turned toward the door. "I have a few things to do, so have your people ready to go in an hour."

When Sy said nothing, she refused to look back at him. It wasn't like he had a choice—he would accompany her to his clan's land.

Still, as she exited the sentry shelter and instructed her people of her plans, Kaya couldn't quite push aside the curiosity nibbling at her mind. Why wouldn't Sy tell her about the letters?

And if he was telling the truth, who had blocked her from receiving them in the first place?

~ ~ ~

Clenching and unclenching his fists, Sy watched Kaya shut the door behind her. Their conversation hadn't gone the way he'd planned. If anything, things were even more fucked up between them. There was no way Kaya was going to let this go. If there was ever a person as stubborn as him—or more, for that matter—it was Kaya Geraldine Alexie.

She seemed sincere in her declaration that she'd never received his letters. His memories of their love wanted to believe her, but Sy the man and former soldier wasn't so easily swayed. When he'd known Kaya, she'd always gotten the information she was after. Even if, and he didn't want to believe it, someone had kept his hundreds of letters from her, she would've found out eventually.

Wouldn't she have?

No. He didn't have time for this. He'd spent years getting over Kaya; he might still be attracted to her, but he couldn't afford to hope she still felt the same. He would do his job and go back to the way things had been for the last decade. End of story.

The doorknob turned and he schooled his face into his usual easygoing appearance. His clan members might've heard raised voices while waiting outside, but he hoped the GreyFire sentry shelter was insulated. He sure as hell didn't want to deal with any of his friends' meddling. His brother and his brother's wife did enough of that.

Dani strutted in and said, "Catch." As he caught the cell phone, she said, "It's just a cheap phone, but Kaya wants you to call your brother. Apparently, we're leaving in an hour."

He opened the cheap flip phone, but didn't dial. Instead, he said, "And just an FYI—Kaya's coming with us."

Aidan frowned. "Why?"

He shrugged. "Beats me. I'm about to pester my brother and see why I have to be the one to show her around."

Aidan grinned. "I hope he makes you do it. I'd love to watch."

Dani plopped down in one of the armchairs. "If that does happen, can I be reassigned? It's going to take me days to get the wolf smell out of my nose as it is."

Sy gave them a look. "Gee, thanks for the support."

Aidan kept grinning and Dani shrugged. If this was how two of his friends and fellow guardians acted, he didn't want to think what his twin brother would do. No doubt, his older-by-five minutes brother would enjoy watching him suffer around his ex-mate-to-be.

He dialed his brother and waited. On the fourth ring, Kian answered. "Hello?"

"Kian, it's Sy."

"I was wondering when the hell you were going to call. Kaya mentioned you punching one of her sentries in the face. I'm assuming you had a reason."

"They were going to send me home, and you'd asked me to stay. Besides, the wolf-bastard was a little too sure of himself. Apparently, any type of 'cat' should be collared and spend his days chasing mice."

He could hear the smile in Kian's voice. "You could've just told him to chase his tail, but that's neither here nor there. When are you coming back? I hope soon. The situation with the strange wolf-shifters has deteriorated."

Pushing aside his irritation at his brother, Sy switched his mind into work mode. "What happened?"

He listened, and once Kian was done explaining, Sy cursed. "I'll see if I can hurry Kaya and get there as soon as possible. With your permission, I'll bring her straight to the main conference room."

"I don't mind her, but I need you to convince her to leave the two wolves accompanying her to wait in the outer waiting area. At this point, my trust only extends so far."

Sy was surprised Kian trusted any of the wolves at all after the poacher incident six years ago, but he would trust his brother's judgment. "Will do."

After hanging up the phone, he looked at Aidan and Dani and answered the question in their eyes. "They just found another infected wolf, but this time, she came with a message."

~~~

Standing across from Erika, Kaya steeled herself for another round of doubts from her second-in-command. And, as expected, her friend had thought of yet another reason why she shouldn't go to DarkStalker's land. "Even if you trust the cougars, I highly doubt they've disinfected the place. The crazy purple-eyed wolves may not be contagious to the cats, but I sure as hell don't want you coming back in a black body bag."

Kaya rolled her eyes. She'd humored her friend long enough. "Erika, I get that part of your job is to protect me, I do. But my word is final, and I'm going. So let's talk about what needs to be done in my absence, okay?"

Erika might be protective, but Kaya was still in charge. By giving a final command, her friend could do nothing but obey. Erika let out a sigh. "Fine. But can I make a suggestion?"

She gave her a wary glance. "What?"

"Before you go, will you let one of our researchers draw blood from each of the three cougar-shifters? I'd feel a whole lot better if we were at least working on a cure, just in case you, or anyone else for that matter, become infected. If the cats are immune, our researchers might be able to find out why."

She nodded. "That's a great idea." One she should've thought of herself if she hadn't been distracted by Sy's revelations inside the sentry shelter.

Kaya picked up her phone and dialed. After contacting Donovan, one of her infectious diseases experts, and telling him about Erika's plan, she hung up and focused back on her friend. "My assistant can give you my schedule for the next few days, but the only major thing that needs to be done is to turn in the paperwork on my desk to the US Bureau of Shifter Affairs. It's due in two days. But don't hesitate to contact me if you have questions or need an answer on any of my other appointments. If I don't pick up my cell, call Kian Murray and he'll find a way to get me the message."

Erika raised her eyebrows. "You seem to trust the cougar-shifter leader more than I would've expected."

Kaya shrugged. "He could've sent the infected wolves out for testing and used the virus against us later. Instead, he asked us for our help. I'd say that's something." Kaya went to the door and looked over her shoulder. "Anything else?"

"Just be careful. You say you're over Sylas Murray, but I'm not convinced. Spending a lot of time with him could end up hurting you in the end."

Erika didn't know the half of it, but she was clan leader and needed to be strong, so she shrugged. "I doubt anything could be worse than him not showing up to our mating engagement ceremony. If he annoys me, then I'll remind him of that fact. He should get cooperative fast after that."

Before Erika could say anything else, Kaya exited the room and headed for her private quarters. Just mentioning that memory made her heart squeeze. While engagement ceremonies were usually jolly, happy times, hers had been as lively as a funeral procession. Almost no one, not even most of her friends, had approved of Sy. Then when the bastard stood her up and left her standing alone, all dressed up and ready to proclaim him as her future mate, everyone had given her looks of pity, as if she'd been a child who had finally realized what everyone else had known all along.

Kaya took a deep breath. Just like back then, she wouldn't cry in front of others. She would be the strong example her clan needed.

In that instant, she decided that even if Sy had written the most groveling and romantic letters in the history of the world, she wasn't sure she would've been able to forgive him. He'd promised to always be by her side, but when she'd needed him most, he had abandoned her.

She reached her quarters, and as she packed her things, she pushed every memory of her and Sy into the corner of her mind and locked them away to focus on the bigger picture. She needed to make sure there wouldn't be an epidemic. She needed to ensure the members of her clan wouldn't die. She also needed to strengthen the truce between DarkStalker and GreyFire.

To accomplish those things, she wouldn't allow anyone to get in her way, most especially a thirty-year-old cougar-shifter with a heart-melting grin.

Chapter Five

Sy decided that spending an hour trapped inside a small, enclosed space with Kaya was his version of a personal hell.

Even with him upfront driving and Kaya in the middle row of seats inside the SUV, he could smell the earthy grass scent that had always driven him crazy as a teenager. He'd never really thought about how memories could be compromised of more than sights or sounds, but right now, his cock remembered what it'd been like to have that scent surrounding him as he'd taken her from the front, from behind, and from any which way they had come up with.

He was just starting to remember where her scent was strongest—when he'd licked between her legs—as they finally reached the turnoff for DarkStalker's public entrance.

Thank fuck. He pulled down the last stretch of dirt road, parked the car, and was out of the SUV as fast as he could undo his seatbelt and open the door.

As he drew in deep lungfuls of fresh air, he heard the sounds of the rest of the shifters disembarking. With his head mostly cleared of the effects of eau de Kaya, he turned around so he could lead the GreyFire leader inside, but spotted his sister-in-law, Trinity Perez-Murray, striding out to greet them.

He narrowed his eyes. Trinity usually didn't greet guests. He wondered what the hell his sister-in-law was up to.

She reached them just as Sy caught up with the group who had gathered to the side of the car. Trin smiled, glanced to Kaya and then back to him. "Care to introduce me?"

Trin knew full well who was standing there, so he merely said, "Trinity, Kaya. Kaya, Trinity."

Trin raised an eyebrow. "I can see why your brother sent me out here. You're grumpy."

He made a noise in his throat, not wanting to challenge his brother's mate in front of the GreyFire wolves. Trinity must've sensed that because she turned toward Kaya and put out a hand. "Excuse my brother-in-law. He's never been very skilled when it comes to tact."

Kaya glanced at him and back. "Believe me; I know that better than most."

Trin laughed. "I suppose you would." Kaya opened her mouth, but Trin beat her to it. "Come. Kian's waiting for you inside." Trinity looked over her shoulder to meet Sy's eyes. "You can show the wolves to the outside waiting area."

Kaya frowned. "I thought Sy was just going to take me to the site of the attack."

Trin glanced to Kaya. "He will, but Kian needs to talk to you first. He has some new information to share."

Jonathan was one of the two wolves who had accompanied Kaya, and he frowned as he said, "You can't expect me to let you take her inside, all alone. I know nothing about you cats, let alone your intentions, and Kaya is too important for me to risk it."

Sy was about to say something when Kaya stared directly at her sentry and said, "I want to hear what Kian Murray has to say. Go with Sy. If something goes wrong, I'll institute the emergency protocol."

Jonathan shut his mouth and nodded. Sy was more than a little impressed. He'd known Kaya was a clan leader, but he'd never really seen her in action.

Then Kaya looked straight at him. "As for you, if you punch my sentry again, I won't be so lenient next time. I might even kick your ass for good measure."

Sy raised an eyebrow and decided to avoid arguing about whether she could beat him or not and said, "Then tell him to behave, or I won't make any promises."

She pointed a finger at him. "Jonathan is levelheaded, which means he would only act out if you provoked him. So don't do it."

"Yes, yes, just go ahead blame me without knowing all the facts. You're good at doing that."

Kaya opened her mouth to reply, but Sy turned and motioned for both the wolves and his own team to follow him. The longer he argued in front of Trinity, the more his sister-in-law would get ideas in her head. Not just any kind of ideas, but matchmaking ideas.

And no way in hell was he going to give Trin any encouragement in that area.

~~~

Kaya watched Sy retreat with her clan members and tried to let his insult roll off her, but failed. She was the one good at blaming him for things? The bastard had abandoned her and nearly cost the truce between the clans.

Fuck him.

Taking a few deep breaths, she willed her face into a neutral expression. This would be her first face-to-face meeting with

DarkStalker's clan leader and she needed a clear mind. If she'd known about the meeting ahead of time—and judging by the look Trinity had given Sy, he should've told her during the ride here—she could've better prepared herself.

Luckily, she liked thinking on her feet and making split-second decisions. She never would've earned the right to be clan leader without those traits.

Satisfied that any sign of her irritation was gone, she turned toward Trinity. The woman was giving her a strange look, and Kaya wondered how much Kian's mate knew about her past with Sy. She decided not to mention it. Instead, she said, "Shall we go?"

But Trinity didn't budge. "You should just fuck him and see what happens."

Kaya blinked. "Excuse me?"

Trinity motioned in the direction Sy had left and back to her. "I'm not denying the two of you have issues, but it's obvious there's some kind of spark still there. Hell, Sy is usually full of grins and smiles, but with you, he's grumpy and irritated. I'd say, at some level, the man still cares for you and he is desperately trying not to show it."

Kaya decided if Trinity wasn't going to stand on formality and politeness, she wouldn't either. "Look, I just met you, and I don't want to disrespect you, but this is clearly my business. Sylas might be your brother-in-law, which means you think the world of him, but he's an asshole, and I don't have the slightest interest in fucking him."

Trinity raised an eyebrow. "Liar."

Kaya put her shoulders back, raised her chin, and gave Trinity her best alpha stare. "Are you going to take me to see Kian or not?"

Trinity shrugged. "I guess, but think about my suggestion. For what it's worth, Sy's never been serious with anyone after you. Sure, he's fucked females occasionally, but never really dated. Just think about it."

"Fine. Whatever. Can we go now?"

Trinity nodded and started walking.

Kaya could see now how Trinity had earned her reputation; the woman said what she wanted, when she wanted, and didn't bother with tiptoeing around an issue. If not for Kian, Kaya could see Trinity taking charge of the cougar-shifter clan.

To be honest, Kaya had a feeling the pair worked together to take care of DarkStalker, which was a rare thing among shifter clans. The cougars, wolves, and bears in the Cascade Mountains were overall a bit more open-minded than the majority of shifter clans in the US. Of the few leaders she'd interacted with, all of whom but one had been male, none of them had ever had their mates sit in on the various conferences calls. Kian had been the sole exception. Nine times out of ten, Trinity had been sitting beside him. True, Trinity had rarely said anything during those calls in the past, but judging from her inability to say anything but what was on her mind, she could understand the necessary caution. A male shifter's pride could be a delicate thing, and not everyone could handle a female poking at it.

As she followed Trinity through the nondescript corridors, she tried to focus on where they were going, but her mind kept drifting to Trinity's words. Surely, the cougar female was wrong about Sy. The man clearly hated her. And even if Kaya's uncle hadn't killed himself three years ago and was alive today, she wasn't sure if she'd ask him about the letters.

Of course, the last of her uncle's closest sentries still resided with GreyFire in the infirmary section. Despite the male being in the beginning stages of Alzheimer's, she might be able to get the truth out of him.

Then Trinity stopped in front of a door and Kaya focused back on the present. She wasn't about to let either herself or her clan down.

After knocking three times, Trinity opened the door and walked inside. Kaya followed to find Kian Murray sitting at a rectangular table, a stack of documents in front of him. When his gaze locked with his mate's, he smiled, his eyes full of love, and the sight made Kaya's heart squeeze. She knew jealously wouldn't accomplish anything, but she wanted what this pair had—love filled with respect and the ability to work as a team.

She doubted she'd ever get it.

Kian's eyes slid from Trinity's to hers and he nodded. "Normally, I'd offer refreshments and shoot the breeze with you before getting down to business, but what I need to say can't wait."

Kaya took the chair across from him and waved a hand. "Trinity has already knocked down the formalities, so just say what you need to say."

His gaze darted to Trinity, and his mate gave a shrug. Satisfied, he looked back to Kaya. "We've found another purple-eyed wolf-shifter this morning."

She leaned forward. "Did Sy know about this? Why wasn't I told?"

Kian said, "I didn't want this information to leak and I told him not to say anything. He was following orders, so don't take it out on him."

Maybe he had changed. Teenage Sylas wouldn't have been able to keep the secret. "And where is this wolf now?"

"The pup's in quarantine."

"Pup as in a baby wolf?"

Kian nodded and his lips set in a grim line. "But that's not the worst of it. The pup came with a flash drive tucked inside a pouch around her neck. After ensuring the flash drive didn't have any type of viruses detrimental to our security systems, one of my techs found a message for you."

"Don't leave me hanging, Kian. What did you find?"

"If you don't refuse all the bids on your latest malaria drug, and keep it off the market indefinitely from humans, a deliberate epidemic will be started on GreyFire's land."

Withdrawing GreyFire's malaria drug was tantamount to financial suicide. She had invested heavily in the research and development and was on the cusp of earning a return on her investment. The threat could be from any number of competitors, and she had a feeling that whoever had sent the message would only keep on blackmailing her clan's efforts. Giving in was not really an option. "Did the message or the flash drive give any hint as to who it was from?"

Kian frowned. "That's the thing. They didn't try to hide their identity. It was from Human Purity."

Human Purity was a mix of religious and secular protesters who believed shifters were no more than animals. They fought against, and occasionally derailed, legislation that gave new rights to shifters. "That doesn't really make any sense. Purity is spending all their time and efforts toward fighting against the proposed human-shifter marriage equality laws in the various states. I have a feeling someone else is using them as a cover."

Kian nodded. "I agree with you. Purity rarely targets a specific clan, let alone a specific species. If you have any clues as to who might want to threaten you, let me know. I want to help track down the bastards for infecting a mere pup."

"As much as I'm glad for your offer of help, why? This affects my clan, and doesn't really benefit yours. If the epidemic succeeded in wiping out GreyFire, most of our land would become yours."

Kian stared at her for a second before he replied, "I know things between GreyFire's and DarkStalker's old clan leaders were tense at best. I also understand how you were embarrassed by my brother."

Trinity interrupted with a warning. "Kian."

He shook his head. "No. I love my brother, but Sy was an idiot all those years ago. He, at least, should've approached Kaya about breaking it off." Trinity huffed and Kian looked back to Kaya. "Despite all of that, I want our truce to be more than a formality written on paper. One day, I want our clans to become almost family-like in their protectiveness of one another, but to do that, you're going to have to forgive Sy. He's one of my top people, and you'll often be forced to be around him and work with him. The question is can you do it? Because if you can, then I have a plan on how to find your blackmailer and maybe save your clan."

~~~

Arms crossed over his chest, Sy stood on the side of DarkStalker's outside waiting area and watched the wolf-shifters in human form. It'd been a long time since he'd had to do babysitting duty, but for once, he was glad for the assignment. The peace and quiet of the forest helped him to clear his head about Kaya.

He only hoped he could remain levelheaded once he was close enough to scent her again.

RECLAIMING THE WOLF

For now, he was more concerned about Trin spending time alone with GreyFire's leader. His sister-in-law had started to make it her mission to find him a mate. Just his luck, she'd try to patch things up between him and Kaya.

And he definitely didn't want that. Or, rather, most of him didn't. His dick wanted to fuck her tight, wet pussy every which way until they were both so exhausted they couldn't do more than lie motionless and breathe.

Shit, okay, he didn't need to be thinking of Kaya's pussy. The woman had broken his heart and dismissed him without a fucking word.

Or had she?

He resisted a growl of frustration. His life had become simple, even predictable, over the last decade, just like he'd wanted. But now a tall, bronze-skinned beauty had turned his world upside-down.

Again.

Fuck. So much for not thinking about her.

Truth be told, if he wanted to be able to focus on his duties and role inside the clan, he really only had two options when it came to Kaya Alexie. He could keep fighting his attraction and the curiosity of what had truly happened between them. Or, he could temporarily put aside his hurt from the past and corner Kaya to see what would happen next.

Thanks to his inner cougar, who was clawing to come out so he could rub his scent all over the wolf-shifter, he was leaning toward the second option.

Not that Sy wouldn't mind rubbing Kaya from head to toe; the woman had always loved a massage. Hell, in the past, she'd usually thanked him afterward by sucking his cock deep into her wet, warm mouth.

As his mind started to relive those memories, his cell phone beeped with an incoming message. He took it out, saw it was from Trinity, and read: "Meeting is over. Bring the wolves to the quarantine observation area. Third one is dead."

Shit. The third wolf-shifter from the attack on his brother had been failing over the last two days, so the death wasn't a surprise. However, if the death was a result of the symptoms of the mysterious virus, they now knew it killed its victims in less than a week. If the infected pup his clan had found this morning was just the first of what was to come, Kaya's clan could be in serious danger.

The thought of Kaya contracting the virus and wasting away into a sick, insane animal didn't sit well with him. No matter what had happened between them, she didn't deserve that fate. Her clan depended on her, and his clan depended on that stability for survival. He would do whatever it took to prevent chaos from happening. The last thing they needed was for the humans to be proven right about shifters being no more than animals.

He sent a quick reply to Trin to let her know he was on his way, and then Sy walked over to Kaya's team and said, "There's news about the infected wolf-shifters and we're needed inside."

Probably because of Kaya's earlier order, they merely nodded and motioned for him to lead the way. He guided them through the "safe" corridors of the mountain used to keep visitors separated from the clan. Once they reached the quarantine viewing room, Sy punched the code into the keypad and the door opened to reveal Kaya, Kian, and Trinity standing in front of a two-way mirror.

They all turned their heads over their shoulders, but it was Kaya who met his gaze first. Even from across the room, the deep brown of her eyes held a guarded look, which he knew meant she was trying to hide strong emotions.

However, unlike when they were younger, Kaya was a leader now, and he knew from working with his brother over the years that a clan leader needed to keep a cool, collected facade no matter how awful something might be. In that instant, he realized that while Kian had Trinity to listen to his true thoughts or to hold him through another death in the clan, Kaya might have no one. Years of holding in her emotions had to be taking a toll on her.

For all he knew, she might be lonely and hurting.

His cougar growled at that thought. They could help her. Why was Sy fighting it?

Not now, he told his cat. They could fight about it later.

Sy headed toward the empty spot next to his brother at the observation window and looked down. He watched as two of DarkStalker's researchers took samples from the dead wolf-shifter, who was still in wolf form. He'd seen his fair share of death while stationed in Iraq, but this particular sight made him uneasy. If they weren't careful, that shifter could easily be Kaya or any of her people.

Sy decided to get more information about the wolf-shifter instead of dwelling on what he might not be able to change. He asked, "What did the wolf-shifter ultimately die of?"

His brother answered, "A combination of dehydration and a secondary infection, both a result of the virus. If the cycle repeats with the new wolf-shifter pup, then we have a week to either find the source and demand a cure, or come up with a cure of our own."

He turned toward his brother. "So which is it going to be?"

Kian motioned for them to move away from the two-way mirror and everyone in the room sat down around the simple table. Kian looked to Kaya. Once she nodded, his brother said, "DarkStalker and GreyFire are teaming up to tackle both. Our clan will reach out to the bears for permission to go onto their land and search all of the nearby mountains for other infected wolf-shifters." Kian looked to Kaya. "You tell him the rest."

Sy moved his gaze to Kaya, who still had an unreadable expression. "My researchers will continue working on a cure and a possible vaccine. Thanks to Kian, they'll have access to any of the cougar-shifters who've interacted with the purple-eyed wolves to study their immunity. As for finding the source, Kian has agreed to watch over both clans while you and I try to find out who is using Human Purity as a cover."

Jonathan the wolf-shifter interjected, "Not alone, surely. As a shifter clan leader, you'll have a target on your back as soon as you step foot in any of the populated human areas."

Kaya gave her clan member a piercing stare. "I don't mind you questioning me, but first, listen to the entire plan before you raise any objections." Her clan member put his hands up in apology and she continued. "The cougars employ humans in most of their DS Engineering locations. While none of their shifters can manage the sites full-time due to the law, Sy and some of his colleagues take one or two week-long trips to check up on things. Sy is due to visit one of their locations in the next few days."

Sylas put it all together. "I'm supposed to visit the IT and software engineer division in Seattle this week. They might be able to tell us where or what company encrypted the flash drive, and maybe even a ballpark location if they can find out the original IP address."

Kaya looked at him and nodded. "Exactly. I have faith in my researchers, but I want to cover every possible solution. If we find out where it originated from, they mostly likely will have a cure in case the virus mutates and starts to infect humans or domestic dogs."

Sy frowned. "But why exactly are you coming with me?"

She gave him a look like it should be obvious. "Because my clan doesn't trust yours. While Kian and I are hoping to change that over time, it will take some convincing. However, if we find something useful, I can simply pick up a phone, call my clan, and tell my wolves what to do and they'll listen."

His brother leaned forward on the table. "Can you handle it, Sylas?"

Kian was really asking him if he could handle working with the woman despite their less-than-happy history.

Well, at least this way he'd have a chance to ask Kaya some questions and get some answers about what had really happened between them.

The hard part would be telling his dick to calm the fuck down.

Still, this was for the benefit of his clan. He could find a way to manage. "Yes, but how are we going to explain her presence? Some of the interns at that location are from DarkStalker and live in the same apartment building as the one I use when I'm in Seattle. If they come upon us, they'll scent she's a wolf straightaway."

Trinity leaned on the table and slowly smiled. "Kaya's going to pretend you two made up and she's your girlfriend again."

Sy blinked before looking to Kaya. "Really?"

She shrugged. "I would do far worse to protect my clan. Besides, it's the best chance we have at making this work."

CHAPTER SIX

A few hours later, Kaya slid into the passenger seat of Sy's SUV, buckled her seatbelt, and tried to ignore the butterflies in her stomach.

She had done a good job of hiding her emotions earlier, both when talking with Kian and in the observation room overlooking the dead wolf-shifter, but spending the next how many days posing as Sy's girlfriend made her nervous. She hadn't lied to Kian; she could do it. However, since shifters were very tactile, affectionate beings, Kaya wasn't sure how she was going to react to Sy caressing her cheek or pulling her close against his side in the presence of others, with his heat and scent surrounding her. Or, even worse, if he decided to nuzzle her neck and start making the human equivalent of a purr.

Her nervousness morphed into something much hotter as she remembered how it had felt to feel Sy's skin next to hers when they'd been naked and tangled in bed sheets.

The driver's side door opened and Kaya barely prevented herself from jumping. Sy tossed a duffel bag into the back and sat down in the driver's seat. She expected him to start the car, but instead, he turned toward her and said, "Are you sure you want to do this? We can find another way."

His doubting her quickly washed away her sexy thoughts of Sy's skin. "Of course I can do this. The safety of my entire clan is at stake."

He sighed. "I know, but I was hoping you had changed your mind."

She studied his face. "Why? You're hiding something from me. If we're to work together, I need to know what it is in case it could jeopardize our investigation."

His gaze flicked up to hers. "Who says I'm hiding anything?"

"I can explain how I know you're hiding something, but I won't bother unless you promise to answer my question after I do." He nodded and motioned his hand for her to continue. She decided to hold nothing back. After turning a little toward him, she said, "You were angry and dickish to me earlier, and now you're all sighs and politeness. Something happened between you stomping off to babysit my wolf-shifters and you sliding into this car. What was it?"

His eyes turned fierce. "Do you really want to know, Kaya? Because I promise you won't like it."

"You haven't truly known me in over a decade. I can take anything you throw my way, so just spit it out already. The longer you hesitate, the less time we have in the city."

He turned in his seat to better face her, and the look of anger and something else she couldn't define in his eyes knocked the wind out of her. She felt the heat of his gaze in places she didn't want to think about.

Her mind might dislike him, but her body very much wanted to get friendly again.

Enough. She was a grown adult, for fuck's sake.

She forced herself to pay attention to his words as he said, "While we might've been apart for more than a decade, I've seen Kian work for years as DarkStalker's clan leader, so I understand you better than you think."

"Kian? What does he have to do with anything?"

"Kian puts up with all kinds of shit and grief to keep the clan together. Hell, we nearly lost him after his leg was shattered by a wild, insane bear-shifter a little over four months ago. But no matter what he goes through or what he has to do to keep the clan together, he always has Trinity.

"It was Trin who brought him back from his bouts of self-pity after the bear attack. She also acts as his confident and—never tell her I said this—as his own personal cheerleader. If things go wrong, he can talk with or fuck my sister-in-law and spring right back. Without her, he would break." He leaned in a few inches. "But today, I realized you have no one. You take on all the responsibilities of your clan and brave whatever needs to be braved with no one to cuddle, talk to, or let alone fuck, at the end of the day. It must be incredibly lonely. Am I right?"

For a second, she could do nothing but stare at him.

Sylas Murray had definitely changed from the cocky teenage boy she'd known. Instead of cheating at a game to claim a kiss or quick fuck, he could easily deconstruct her role and the reasons behind her self-imposed isolation, and do it in less than a day.

The boy had become a man, and to be honest, she wasn't sure what to make of it. Hell, the more she talked with him, the more she started to believe she didn't know him at all anymore.

And that could be very, very dangerous. If she wasn't careful, she could slip and start to fall for this more mature version of him, a version who might be her equal.

She cleared her throat and managed to say, "You expect me to believe you got all of that from a few hours in my company?"

He leaned even closer, but Kaya maintained her position. She would not retreat from him. "Yes, but that's not the only reason for my behavior. Do you want to know what else changed?"

Her heart rate ticked up. Her voice was low when she asked, "What?"

He raised a hand and traced a finger down her cheek. His touch was rough and warm, and she barely resisted shivering. Somewhere in her mind she knew she should push him away. Yet a part of her yearned for a male's touch, and her touch-starved wolf howled inside her head at finally getting it.

Whatever she'd done over the years to convince herself she was no longer attracted to Sylas Murray vanished.

As she battled the need to either touch him in return or to bolt from the car, Sy's voice was low and husky, demanding her attention as he said, "I decided to stop fighting my attraction to you."

Kaya couldn't help but say, "What?"

He moved his finger from her cheek to her ear. As he traced the outer edges, his touch heated her whole body, making her pussy ache. Out of nowhere, she imagined what it would feel like to have his hard, long cock pound into her from behind as she bent over the hood of the car, and wetness rushed straight to her core.

Sy might've done many things wrong when he was younger, but even then, he'd known how rough and hard she liked it. No one after had come close to reading her needs, especially after she'd become clan leader. All of the wolves had been afraid of upsetting her, which had resulted in them treating her like some goddamn porcelain doll who would break at the first sign of strength.

But never Sy. Oh, that man knew just how rough to be without hurting her.

Kaya swallowed. *Fuck*. This was bad, very bad. If she didn't do something, she'd be jumping him in no time flat.

Sy moved to her ear and his breath was hot against her skin as he whispered, "I can smell that you're attracted to me too. How about a quick fuck, with no strings attached, to ease both of our tension? We'll both be more productive once this burning need to fuck each other like rabbits is out of the way."

Damn the man and his nose. But as much as she didn't want to admit it, he was right—getting the tension out of the way would allow them to work more efficiently. Or, so she told herself.

Trinity's words came back to her. *You should just fuck him and see what happens.*

She hesitated a second before realizing she had earned this. They could afford to delay their departure by half an hour. Especially since she'd been tired of the porcelain treatment and had given up trying to have sex with anyone inside her clan. Sy was willing, and despite however he might've changed over the last decade, she doubted he was any less thrilling when naked.

If anything, he was probably better.

It was time for Kaya to start taking care of herself; an orgasm or two might relieve some of her worry and stress about what might happen to her clan. That way she could give one-hundred and ten percent toward tracking down the source.

Besides, he'd said no strings attached. That was an offer she couldn't pass up.

She raised a hand and placed it on his chest, disappointed that the material prevented her from touching his skin. She heard his breath hitch, and that sealed it—she was doing this.

She reached behind her with her free hand and found the handle. However, if she was doing this, it was going to be her way.

She pushed against Sy's chest and he moved back. Once she could see his eyes, she smiled and said, "Okay, but only if you can catch me."

Then she opened the door and dashed into the forest.

~~~

Sy hadn't expected her to say yes, but as Kaya ran into the forest, he decided he sure as hell wasn't going to pass up this chance, especially now that he had to chase her.

He scrambled out of the car and headed in the direction Kaya had been seconds earlier. About ten feet into the trees, he stopped and took in a deep inhale until he could pick out her earthy grass scent. He didn't need to shift to catch her like he'd done in his youth. One of the things he'd mastered while working in the Shifter Division of the US Army had been how to track down a target.

He moved as quickly as he could while keeping his noise to a minimum. He tried to focus solely on his prey, but his chest still burned from the touch of her hand. It'd taken every ounce of restraint he'd possessed not to pull her close and kiss the living shit out of her plump, hot, fuckable mouth.

Maybe when he caught her, she'd take his cock into her mouth at the same time as he tongued her sweet, wet pussy.

Judging from what he'd scented in the car, she was already dripping for him.

His cock pulsed and Sy decided he'd never catch her unless he focused. With herculean effort, he banished any and all images that involved Kaya naked and at his mercy.

He continued the hunt, her scent getting stronger before it disappeared completely in front of a waterfall with a small pool beneath it. He eyed the water cascading over rocks to his left, and smiled. He'd used that hiding spot himself as a boy.

He moved out of the line of the sight of the little cave hidden behind the waterfall and inched to the entrance. One second ticked by, then ten. She had to know he was near, but the anticipation would only make her more hot and needy for his touch.

Unable to restrain himself any longer, he dashed into the crack behind the waterfall. It took half a second for him to spot Kaya inside the cave before he moved and pinned her against the wall. The heat of her skin burned through the wet fabric of both their shirts, her nipples hard against his chest. Later, was going to suck those little points deep, knowing Kaya would moan and squirm at his attentions.

For now, he leaned his head in until his lips were a hairbreadth away from hers and whispered, "Gotcha."

Her heated gaze bore into his. Neither of them blinked. Her breath was hot against his lips, but he didn't kiss her. Not yet.

Instead, he gripped her wrists with his hands and raised them above her head. When she didn't fight him, he put himself on guard. Either she was so horny she would do anything to get his dick inside her, or she was acting complacent so he would underestimate her.

Reclaiming the Wolf

After securing her wrists with one hand, he used the other to trace her cheek, the side of her jaw, and finally her warm, soft bottom lip. Kaya broke her silence and whispered, "Stop teasing me. You promised to fuck me, so why the delay?"

He smiled. "Because you stopped trying to run from me. You knew I'd easily find you inside this cave." He pressed his erection against her stomach, loving the hard-yet-soft feel of her tall, toned body. "I never want you to hide your skills and abilities from me, and since you didn't give me a true challenge, you're going to strip and let me lap my fill of your sweet pussy before my cock goes anywhere near it."

Despite the fact the scent of her arousal grew stronger, she narrowed her eyes and said, "You mentioned nothing about foreplay. I just want your hard dick inside me. Now."

He leaned in and nuzzled her cheek. "Patience."

Before she could reply, he took her lips in a swift, rough kiss. When he moved away, Kaya rubbed against him as best she could with her arms restrained. She whispered, "Again."

He complied, and nibbled her bottom lip before pushing his tongue inside her hot mouth. Kaya wasn't one to let him take complete control, and she met him stroke for stroke as she moved her lower body against his. If he didn't stop the vixen, he'd come before he'd ever taken off his jeans.

He leaned all of his weight against her as he took the kiss deeper, their teeth clashing as they each fought for control. *Fuck yes.* This is what he'd missed—a woman who wasn't afraid to take what she wanted.

He eased his chest a little from hers, his free hand moving to her breasts. As he pinched and rolled her nipple through her shirt and bra, Kaya moaned into his mouth. While he loved the feel and taste of her mouth, he needed more. Much more.

He broke the kiss but continued to play her with her taut nipples. Kaya's breathing was fast now, and with a hard pinch, she moaned.

"Kaya, look at me."

She opened her eyes. They were heavy with desire—for him. She might be able to go all alpha leader stoic when they were surrounded by other people, but right here, with just the two of them, she didn't hide her emotions. For a brief second, he wanted her to act like this always with him. Then he quickly pushed that thought aside. Sex was one thing, but having a relationship was quite another.

He moved his free hand from her breast and slid it inch by inch down her stomach, stopping at the waistband of her jeans. He ran his finger under her shirt, and Kaya squirmed. She was still ticklish there.

"Don't even think of tickling me, Sylas."

He moved his finger again and she tried to jerk away. "Only if you take off your pants and underwear."

She attempted to glare, but then he tickled her again and she fought off a laugh. When he stopped, she managed to say, "Fine, but only if you take off your shirt."

He gave her one last rough kiss before he released her wrists. She waited with an expectant look as he tugged his wet t-shirt over his head. Both his ego and his cock drank in the female appreciation in her eyes as she devoured the defined muscles of his shoulders and chest before resting on the bulge between his thighs.

Under her scrutiny, his dick let out a drop of precum.

He cleared his throat, and Kaya went to work. He tried not to laugh as she tugged at her wet jeans, the suckers not wanting to come off. When she finally succeeded, she tossed them on the far side of the cave before doing the same with her underwear. She was about to remove her t-shirt when he moved to stop her hands with his. "Don't. Your breasts will distract me from focusing on your beautiful, pink pussy."

She huffed, "Sy, you don't have to use fake pretty words. Just give me an orgasm and I'll be happy."

He framed her face with his hands and caressed her cheeks with his thumbs. "They aren't fake words." He kissed her and tugged at her bottom lip with his teeth before he released it. "Now, spread your legs."

She shook her head as she widened her stance, and he slowly ran his hands down her body until he was kneeling before her. He leaned forward and breathed deep. "Yes, you still have the best smelling pussy I've ever known." He opened his eyes and looked up. "And now I'm going to devour you."

~ ~ ~

As Kaya look down into the molten-green eyes of the gorgeous man at her feet, she felt two things she hadn't felt in a long while. She felt both pretty and desired.

To be honest, she hadn't realized just how much she'd missed this sort of intimacy. Hell, she'd hopped around on one leg trying to get off her wet jeans, and Sy had barely kept from laughing. To most people, it was no big deal. But to a leader who always had to be strong, or sympathetic, or comforting, or any of the other million things her position required, it was a relief to just be an imperfect woman and not care about how her every action would be judged.

Sy rubbed the sensitive skin of her inner thigh and she forgot about everything else but the friction of his hand. "Kaya, you're thinking too hard. I think I need to fix that."

She didn't feel comfortable enough to say, "Yes, make me forget about everything but your tongue." Instead, she lowered a hand to his hair and pushed him toward her core. "Well, then hurry up."

He grinned and her breath hitched. This older Sylas might have a scar on his chin and wrinkles at the corner of his eyes, but age had been good to him.

When he lifted her leg, she pushed her free hand against the rock wall behind her to balance as he maneuvered her leg over his shoulder. Once the skin on the back of her knee made contact with his hot, hard shoulder, he leaned in and licked her from slit to clit, and she forgot about everything else but the feel of his wet tongue's assault on her nerves.

As he licked and lapped, his two-day-old whiskers rubbed against her thighs and swollen pussy lips. She loved the friction of his scruff against her sensitive skin. Later, she wanted to feel it rubbing against her breasts, too.

As Sy sucked her swollen clit between his teeth, she tightened her grip in his hair. But damn the man, he pulled back and focused on nibbling her swollen folds before thrusting his tongue in her pussy. While not his cock, her inner wolf howled in approval at the intimate touch.

She tilted her hips in encouragement, greedy for what else he could give her. He teased a little more with his tongue before he nipped her clit, and her legs buckled. Only the wall and Sy's shoulder kept her standing.

He continued his relentless assault, sucking and swirling with his tongue, and Kaya felt the tension build. If he would only bite her one more time...as if he could read her thoughts, he bit her. Hard. Pleasure coursed through her body, increasing with each small spasm as she orgasmed.

Sy gave one last long lick before his hands moved from her hips to up under her shirt. He pulled down her bra and grabbed her breasts. He squeezed, and since they were heavy and sensitive from her orgasm, Kaya closed her eyes to enjoy the feeling of his warm, rough hands. As he squeezed again, her pussy throbbed, not caring that she'd just had an orgasm; it wanted his cock.

"Sy, please..."

He moved her leg to the dirt floor of the cave, stood up, and released her breasts. He stared a second into her eyes and the world went still. She could barely contain her curiosity at what he'd do next.

Leaning down, he kissed her long and deep, the taste of herself on his tongue arousing her even more. She grabbed his shoulders and pulled him close. She could feel his hot, hard dick through his jeans, the bulge a teasing feeling against her stomach. She moved her hips, and at his growl, desire shot between her legs.

He pulled away and both the woman and the wolf parts of her resisted a whimper. It had been too long since they'd had this kind of skin-to-skin contact. They were starved for touch.

Then, without ever taking his eyes from hers, Sy unbuttoned his jeans and her inner wolf retreated, aware of what was coming. As the zipper went down, Kaya licked her lips in anticipation.

CHAPTER SEVEN

Sy was still trying to get over how good Kaya tasted when her little pink tongue darted out to lick her lips. His cock pulsed. His inner cougar was impatient to fuck the female in front of him. Then she'd carry their scent and keep the other males away. At least, for a little while. Then he'd have to fuck her again.

He pushed his cat to the back of his mind and focused on Kaya. When he finally freed his cock from his jeans, Kaya's gaze went to his dick curled up against his belly. He nearly came as her eyes took in every inch of him. The scent of her arousal grew even stronger and was now all but filling the cave.

He needed to be naked. Now.

He was only marginally better at getting out of his wet jeans than Kaya, but since he'd gone commando, he didn't have to worry about any underwear. He took his dick in hand and forced himself to look at Kaya's face. Another drop of precum came out at the hunger and desire he saw there.

He'd been patient and given her a mind-blowing orgasm, but he was done waiting. He wanted to fuck her.

He moved over to her, grabbed her hips, and pulled her flush against him. Thankfully, she'd removed her shirt and bra and they were now skin to skin. Every inch of him now pressed against her felt as if it were on fire.

Leaning down, he nuzzled her cheek. "Normally, I would spin you around so I could fuck both your hot, wet pussy and your tight little ass, but we don't have enough time if we're to stay on schedule." He moved one of his hands to her right ass cheek and squeezed. "But even if I only have time to fuck your pussy, I still plan to make it very rough and very hard." He released her. "Choose your position."

Kaya reached between them and gripped his cock. Sy drew in a breath as she squeezed. Hard.

"Hard and rough? Yes. But ordering me around?" She squeezed harder. "No."

He groaned. "Kaya."

She smiled. "Good. I think you understand me now." She moved and kneeled on the ground. As she bent down on all fours and lifted her ass in the air, he whispered, "Thank fuck," before he moved behind her. He might be part human, but his cougar side liked nothing more than to take a female from behind.

No doubt Kaya's inner wolf felt the same.

He positioned his cock at her swollen wet entrance, but didn't thrust. Kaya was convinced this was a one-time deal, and as much as his mind and inner cat was already shouting "no fucking way," he needed to show he cared about her future. Unlike when he'd been a nineteen-year-old jerk and had used less-than-reliable methods of avoiding pregnancy, he would be a responsible male this time. He caressed the smooth, tan skin of her lower back and asked, "Are you on birth control?"

"Yes." She rubbed against his cock. "Now fuck me."

With one hard thrust, he complied.

Her head dropped and she groaned. He grabbed her hips and started moving, her moans increasing with each thrust. "You're so damn tight." In and out. "And so wet."

"Sy, harder."

First he slapped her ass before increasing his pace to the point his flesh started slapping against hers. He wondered if he was pounding her too hard, but as Kaya continued to moan and say his name, he decided she was fine. She might be female, but she was anything but delicate.

He reached around and grabbed one of her heavy, swinging breasts. They fit perfectly into his palm and he squeezed. Kaya arched her back, and never giving up his rhythm, he released her breast to take hold of her nipple and twist.

Kaya arched her back even more as she cried out. "Yes, yes. Do it again."

He did and her pussy clenched around his cock.

Fuck, he was close. But he wasn't a selfish bastard, so he moved his hand from her nipple to her clit and rubbed the swollen flesh. He increased the pressure and demanded, "Come for me, Kaya-love."

He pinched and she let out a cry as her tight pussy gripped his cock and squeezed. All the while he thrust harder, loving the feel of the squeezing with the pull of his skin as he moved back and pushed forward.

The tingle at the base of his spine was too much, and he thrust to the hilt, letting his hot semen fill her pussy. When the last drop was wrenched from him, Sy leaned against Kaya's back, put his arms around her waist, and kissed the back of her neck.

As her feminine scent filled his nose and her heat warmed his chest, he realized holding her just felt...right. He'd been hurt by her actions from all those years ago, but when he put that anger aside, he felt the pull Kaya had always had on him. He was starting to think they might fit better now than they ever had when they were younger.

RECLAIMING THE WOLF

Of course, that was a dangerous thought, but he ignored the warning bells inside his head. He squeezed her waist and decided, fuck it. He was going to pursue her and find out if he was right. No matter what happened, it would be better than always wondering 'what if.'

~ ~ ~

Kaya's wolf reveled in the feel of a naked man at her back, holding her close in his arms. Touch was something the animals in them craved, but Kaya had ignored the need for too long. Or, more likely, while she'd had touch, she hadn't had the right kind. She was an alpha female and her wolf would only be happy with an alpha male's touch. Sy might be outside the hierarchy of her clan, but as DarkStalker's second-in-command, he was most definitely an alpha. Given the chance, he could soothe both the woman and the wolf.

But then Kaya remembered the dead wolf-shifter she'd seen a few hours ago, and instantly felt guilty. Here she was, dreaming about having a man to cuddle and comfort her, and all the while, another infected wolf could be roaming the mountains, infecting one of her clan members right this instant.

She was clan leader first, and she could never forget that.

Kaya lifted one of her hands from the ground and found Sy's hands at her waist. He tried to lace his fingers with hers, but she grabbed his fingers and tugged at his hand. "Let me go, Sy."

For a second, he did nothing, but then he released her. As he moved away, she felt his cock slide out of her. She tried not to notice the empty ache with him gone. Instead, she stood up and brushed the dirt off her hands and knees.

She squared her shoulders and turned around. She hated how Sy had an unreadable expression on his face.

Oh well, best to act as if she hadn't just had one of the best fucks of her life. "We should quickly rinse off and get back to the car or we'll never make it to Seattle before midnight."

Sy stared at her for a second before he said, "Okay."

Then he picked up his clothes and walked out of the cave without another word.

That was exactly what she'd wanted him to do, so why did she feel more than a little pissed off at his actions? For a few seconds, she'd felt as if Sy had wanted to keep her for more than one quick fuck. But either she'd misjudged him or he was letting her not-so-subtlety know that if she wanted him again—or anything more—she'd have to voice it out loud.

She gathered her clothes, squeezed through the crack that served as the cave's entrance, and passed through the cascading waterfall. Stepping into the small, cold pool of water at her feet, she looked around and noticed Sy was gone.

Well, then. She felt a little hurt at his "fuck and leave" method, but at least he'd given her two mind-blowing orgasms.

As she quickly washed between her legs, the tenderness of her skin brought back the memory of her on her hands and knees with Sy pistoning behind her. She had missed that kind of closeness, and by extension, trust. If her inner wolf didn't trust him, it never would've allowed him to take her from behind.

She wasn't quite sure how to interpret that.

Deciding it was best not to dwell on that fact for too long, she stepped out of the pool and wrung the water from her hair. She was about to start her trek back to the car when Sy reappeared and tossed something at her. She caught the t-shirt as

Sy said, "Since we were going to pick up some clothes for you in the city, that'll have to suffice for now."

For some reason, the fact he'd only left so he could fetch her one of his t-shirts to wear made her feel happy.

Shit. So much for being a mature and collected clan leader. All it took was some great sex for her to start acting like a teenager.

She resisted the urge to lift the shirt up to her nose to breathe in his scent, and instead, simply tossed it over her head. Since she was nearly as tall as him, the shirt barely covered her pussy and ass, but at least it would protect her breasts and sensitive skin from the bushes and trees of the forest.

She forced her gaze upward, and damn the man, he was still stoic. Fine. If he was going to act like nothing had happened, so would she. That might actually work best. They both needed to focus on tomorrow.

"Thanks," Kaya said before heading back to the car.

~~~

The next morning, Sy stood in the kitchen of the apartment DarkStalker rented in Seattle for visits. He stared at the coffee machine and willed it to finish brewing. He'd had a hell of a night, and only caffeine was going to get him through the day.

Kaya had spent their drive to Seattle replying to emails and doing who the hell knew what else on her smartphone, but he hadn't minded her purposefully ignoring him. After all, he was still trying to figure out what he was going to do. He hadn't imagined her going soft in his arms yesterday, nor had he misjudged the longing in her eyes last night. She was lonely, plain and simple. The problem was, she would rather be tortured than admit it.

She took her job as clan leader seriously. He would never try to change that, but whether she knew it or not, the woman needed to learn to relax and lean on at least one other person. Otherwise, within a few years, she might have a nervous breakdown. Not because she was female; no, because he'd heard of it happening to other mateless clan leaders in the past.

Yet, if Kaya had someone to lean on, she would probably become even stronger and more determined than ever to change some of the patriarchal shifter ways to the benefit of her clan. And to be honest, the more he started to imagine himself as the person she turned to, the more he wanted it to be true.

Yes, shit had gone down between them when they'd been younger, but last night he'd realized that none of the other women he'd ever held or fucked had fit as perfectly as Kaya Alexie. She was smart, sexy, stubborn, and would be able to keep up with him in the bedroom. And most of all, when she didn't try to hide behind the emotionless mask of a leader, she was extremely fun to provoke.

He had planned on devising a strategy to get her naked with him again last night, but instead, he'd spent the time replaying every sexual encounter he'd ever had with her. Even now, his cock was hard and hurting for relief. One night with Kaya would never be enough.

The coffee machine chimed it was done and he took out two mugs. After pouring milk into one and spooning sugar into the other, he filled them with coffee, and headed for the second bedroom. He banged the door with his elbow and received a muffled, "Come in."

RECLAIMING THE WOLF

Maneuvering one cup to rest between the wall and his hip, he opened the door, and then grabbed the cup again. He stepped inside to see Kaya lying on the bed, her hair mussed around her face as she rubbed her eyes with the back of her hands. He couldn't help but smile at the sight. "Good morning, sunshine."

She lowered her hands and glared. He laughed before lifting one of the cups of coffee. "I come bringing caffeine."

Her brows eased and she sat up. "Then hurry up and give it to me. Otherwise, you'll be dealing with the grumpy as hell version of me."

He didn't move. "I would think after two orgasms last night, you'd be a little more relaxed."

He waited to see if she'd brush the topic aside or address it head on. When she picked up a pillow, he knew she'd brush it aside. "Give me the damn coffee, Sylas, or this pillow is going to make friends with your face."

Since they had an appointment with one of his contacts in about an hour, he decided to pursue the topic later. "Okay, okay." He walked over and handed her the mug with milk.

She took a sip and smiled. "It's perfect. I can't believe you remembered how I like it about half coffee and half milk."

He sipped his own coffee. "I was once a caring boyfriend, if you remember."

She looked at him askance. "I remember you getting the coffee ready as soon as you woke up to avoid dealing with my grumpiness."

He shrugged. "Hey, there's nothing wrong with self-preservation."

He waited for her to argue, but Kaya remained quiet. Neither the man nor the cougar liked her silence, so he decided to stick to a safer topic. "I've set up a meeting with our most trusted

81

man inside DS Engineering. He was sort of a hacker as a teenager, but gave it up to go to college."

"How long have you known him?"

"I've been acting as a liaison for the software engineer division for four years now, and Dave has been there from my very first day. I also know if there's anything he can't do, he knows someone who can."

Kaya nodded. "Fine. Since Trinity made some calls and had clothes delivered here for me before we arrived last night, I just need a shower. Give me five minutes to finish my coffee, and another twenty to get ready."

He gave her face and then the gentle slope of her breasts underneath one of his shirts a thorough perusal. "You sure you don't want some help in the shower?"

"Sylas."

He met her eyes again. "Whenever you use my full name, I know to leave it be." He moved to the doorway and decided to take a chance. "But I'm going to let you know now, Kaya Alexie, that once we ensure your clan's safety, I'm going to pursue you full-on. I spent all last night thinking of every way I want to fuck you, and I plan on recreating each and every scenario."

She paused with her coffee cup halfway to her mouth and he could smell her arousal. One night wasn't going to be enough for her, either.

With that, he smiled and shut the door behind him.

The words had just come out, but he was glad he said them. With any luck, she'd now think about him in the shower.

CHAPTER EIGHT

Since becoming clan leader, Kaya had rarely had the opportunity to leave GreyFire's land. In truth, it had been about two years since she'd last been in Seattle, and she hadn't been able to see much when they'd arrived late last night. Now, in broad daylight, she could see and drink in the eclectic mix of modern glass buildings nestled right next to old brick ones. Since it was a rare blue-sky day, she could also see the beautiful mountains to both the west and east of the city with the dark blue water of the Puget Sound in between. Sure, she lived in the Cascade Mountains to the east, but there was something almost magical about seeing the snow-topped peaks at this distance.

All too soon, Sy turned their car into an underground parking garage beneath one of the office buildings and the sights of downtown were replaced with a low-lit concrete contraption. She might live inside a mountain, but at least her den had ample lighting and air circulation. Her inner wolf itched to get back outside.

Sy turned off the ignition and Kaya couldn't exit the car fast enough. She moved toward Sy, but as soon as she was within arms' reach, he hauled her up against his chest. She gasped at the hard muscles pressed against her breasts and her nipples betrayed her by going hard. She looked up into his eyes and her voice was breathy to her own ears as she asked, "What are you doing?"

Sy gave a wicked smile and squeezed her tighter against him. Then he leaned down to her ear and whispered, "You're supposed to play the part of my girlfriend, remember? Since anyone could be watching, we can't turn it on and off. Shifters like touch, and when we're in public, I'm going to keep you glued to my side."

She was about to give him a harsh whisper scolding when he bit her earlobe and she drew in a breath. As he licked at the bite, her heart rate kicked up and warmth spread through her body. He bit her again, and she grasped the shirt on his chest as wetness rushed between her legs.

Damn it, her body responded far too easily to his.

Sy growled and stopped his attentions to whisper, "I can smell you, Kaya. Tell me I can fuck you again later, or I'll never be able to concentrate during our upcoming meeting."

The images she'd had in the shower of Sy fucking her against the cool tiles while hot water cascaded over their joined bodies came rushing back. Before she could stop herself, she said, "How can you still do this to me, and make me want you? By all rights, I should still hate you for standing me up at our engagement ceremony ten years ago."

Sy nuzzled her cheek. "Did you ever think maybe all of that was supposed to happen, and only through our mistakes and maturing apart, could we fit together better in the future?"

She pushed against his chest and Sy leaned back. As she stared into his green eyes, she wished she could fall for his pretty words and see what happened, but too many people were counting on her right now. Whatever the hell was going on between them would have to wait. "We need to go or we'll be late for our meeting."

Reclaiming the Wolf

His jaw set in a firm line, but then he leaned down and placed a gentle kiss on her lips. The touch was fleeting, and she barely registered it before his warmth was gone. Sy released her and held out a hand. "Then let's go."

She put her hand in his, loving the feel of his strong, rough hand gripping her own. She yearned to have those rough hands roam her body before pulling her close into a tight embrace. But no matter how much she wanted it, she had a job to do first.

~~~

As Sy guided Kaya out of the parking garage and out onto the street, he tried not to smile. Sure, Kaya hadn't jumped into his arms and professed undying love, but she'd admitted to wanting him. That was a start.

And his cougar approved.

Soon they reached the designated meeting area on Third Avenue. After crossing the street, they ascended the small flight of steps to an open plaza strewn with old bits of the building that had once stood there. He wasn't entirely sure what purpose they served, but humans seemed attached to their architecture, so he wasn't going to question it too thoroughly.

He pulled Kaya over to the wall on the side of the plaza, which doubled as a tall planter, to partially obscure them from view. He leaned back, spun Kaya around, and pulled her against his chest. Before she could say a word, he whispered, "Your height gives away that you're a shifter. I can get away with it, because some human males are tall, but you can't. Leaning against me helps give the illusion you're shorter than you are. The less attention we draw to ourselves, the better."

She harrumphed, but nodded. His inner cougar purred at the heat of her of body against his, as well as her sweet grass scent filling his nose. The cat wanted to come out, rub against Kaya's legs, and try to earn an ear-scratching, but he wasn't about to shift in the middle of downtown Seattle. People here were more accepting than most places, but there were shifter haters everywhere. A shifter who let down their guard was most likely a dead one.

He kept watch on the comings and goings of people, looking in particular for his human contact. Thankfully, Kaya kept silent and never tried to pull away while they waited for the human to arrive. If anything, she relaxed more against him as he squeezed her tighter, enjoying the feel of her body in his arms.

Less than five minutes later, his thirty-year-old, slightly overweight contact ascended the stairs to the plaza. Not wanting to draw attention to himself, he kept quiet. Dave knew where to find him.

His contact turned and headed straight for him. He looked a little confused at the woman in Sy's arms since Sy had always come alone in the past, but smart man that he was, he didn't question it. He held out a small piece of paper and Kaya took it. She opened the scrap and he read over her shoulder, "Markgen."

Sy looked back up to Dave. "Are you sure?"

His contact nodded. "The encryption was fairly easy to break, if you knew what to look for."

Markgen was one of the biggest pharmaceutical companies in the State of Washington. Getting into their headquarters was going to take some hard-ass finagling. Sy would probably have to trade in every favor he had.

He nodded at Dave. "Thanks. I owe you one."

Reclaiming the Wolf

Dave eyed Kaya again and Sy resisted the urge to growl at another man's eyes on his female.

Wait, since when had he started to think of Kaya as his female again? He was going to have to watch that. Just because he'd fucked her didn't mean he had a claim on her. According to shifter tradition, clan leaders had to make a claim first, and Kaya hadn't done so. But he was working on that part.

Sy thanked his contact and waited until he was out of earshot before he whispered into Kaya's ear, "Since I don't have to visit DS Engineering's branch location until tomorrow, I think we should grab some food and head back to the apartment to exchange information and come up with a plan."

She nodded. "Sounds good."

Kaya was tense as she rose up and moved out of his arms, and he started to get the feeling the wolf was keeping something from him. DarkStalker had little involvement with companies like Markgen since the pharmaceutical company had never contracted DarkStalker for work, but GreyFire's bread and butter were vaccines and new drug therapies. They had probably worked with the company many times over.

The only question was whether she would trust him with the inner workings of her clan's business interests or not.

He moved to Kaya's side, placed a hand at her waist, and urged her back to the parking garage. The sooner he got them back to the apartment, the sooner he could try to find out what was bothering Kaya. He didn't want her to face this alone.

Sy tried to think of the best way to approach this. He'd worked with his brother for years, and while he was still getting to know Kaya's style, she put her heart and soul into her clan, just like his brother. No doubt, there were some similarities in their work ethics.

Of course, no matter what he did, the decision of whether or not to share secrets would ultimately be hers. He could only hope she would let him in again because both the man and the cougar desperately wanted to understand the older, more mature version of Kaya Alexie.

~~~

If a possible outbreak hadn't been enough to worry about, now Kaya had to decide what to do about Markgen.

The big pharma company was her clan's biggest research partner. Due to the restrictive laws about shifters, there was a limit to what Kaya's wolves could and could not do when it came to the final stages of drug research. Any clinical trials on humans had to be conducted by humans, and since only a select few companies would even work with shifters, Kaya's choices had been few.

Markgen was known for being shifter-friendly. She'd set up a collaborative project just after she'd become clan leader, nearly three years ago. She, and her head of research, had started to trust them.

But if Sy's contact was correct and Markgen was responsible for the wolf-shifter virus, she'd have to cut all ties and risk bankrupting her clan.

Since they were now back in the car, Kaya closed her eyes and massaged her temples. If she could only shift and go for a run, she could clear her head and think of how to handle this situation. Letting her wolf run free was, hands down, the best way for her to de-stress and focus.

However, going for a run in the middle of a big city wasn't an option. Sy probably knew of the local shifter-safe areas where they could run free, but that would require asking him about it. So far, he'd been respecting her wishes to stay silent. She was grateful for that, but on the other hand, she knew he wouldn't let her go anywhere until he had answers. Curiosity had never killed the cat next her, and probably never would.

Opening her eyes, Kaya sighed. It was best to get this conversation over with now. "I'm guessing you want to know about Markgen?"

Sy glanced over and then back to the road. "Since it probably involves a few of your clan secrets, I was letting you think about what you could share."

Damn. She was starting to understand what he'd said earlier about knowing what she was like from his years of working with his brother. Her wolf howled in approval at the cougar not trying to take charge. Because if he did, they would have to fight him, and her wolf really didn't want to fight him unless it was necessary. He made them feel good. The wolf wanted more sex, and soon.

Coaxing her inner wolf to be quiet, Kaya focused back on the situation on hand. "GreyFire has two possibly lucrative clinical trials going on—one for a malaria drug and the other for a cancer drug. The short story is that both drugs use bits of shifter DNA to fight off the diseases, and only a handful of human companies will work with drugs like that."

Sy nodded in understanding and she continued, "Right now, Markgen is in the final stage of testing both drugs. The results have been promising, and we might even have FDA approval by next year for the malaria one."

The cougar-shifter glanced at her. "Do you think Markgen wants to patent the drug themselves?"

"It's possible. With approval, it could be extremely profitable, even with our plan to donate large amounts of the drug to the hardest hit countries for free."

Sy turned into the apartment's parking garage. "I bet Markgen doesn't like that last part. If they removed your clan from the equation, what would happen?"

She'd had similar suspicions. "If GreyFire was completely annihilated, they would own all the rights to both of the trials as well as the drugs."

Sy turned off the car and turned toward her. "What do you want to do? I could tap my contacts and trade some favors to get some inside information on Markgen, but I don't want to jeopardize your clan's finances in case we're wrong."

She studied the man sitting across from her. Judging by the tension of his body, his instincts were screaming to act and take care of Markgen. Yet here he was, asking her what should be done.

Sy's words from earlier popped into her head. *Did you ever think maybe all of that was supposed to happen, and only through our mistakes and maturing apart, could we fit together better in the future?*

She was starting to think he had a point. With every hour that passed, he showed how much he could support and help her without trying to dominate her. Maybe—just maybe—they could try again. But first, she needed the truth about their past. If he gave it to her, she would risk telling him a few clan secrets. If she couldn't confide the secrets to him, he couldn't really help her when it came to Markgen.

Before she could change her mind, Kaya asked, "What did your letters say all those years ago?"

Sy blinked. "You want to talk about that now?"

She nodded. "Before I can start divulging more clan secrets, I want the truth from you, as a display of trust."

He searched her eyes for a second before he said, "Mostly I asked for you to forgive me, and if by some miracle you did, I'd do anything to earn back your love, even if it meant challenging your uncle. I was half a man without you."

At the fierce look in Sy's eyes, Kaya stopped breathing. She wanted to believe the look was because he still cared for her, but she pushed that thought aside. She needed to hear the rest. "When did you start sending them?"

"As soon as I finished boot camp. Unless I was on a mission or incapacitated, I sent one every day."

She searched his eyes. They were open and honest. For some reason, both she and her inner wolf believed him.

Once they'd dealt with Markgen and took care of this virus, she would ask her uncle's old sentry for the truth. Her uncle, Frances Alexie, had never approved of her choice of mate. And after trying to clean up the mess he'd made of her clan with his egotistical ambitions, it would fit with his character to hide Sy's letter from her so he could ensure they'd never reconcile.

She had focused so long on the hurt and pain of Sy's actions that she'd never bothered to look for any other explanation of his complete silence. Neither one of them could change the past, but she could try for a clean slate from this point forward. She took a deep breath and said, "I promise you, Sylas, I never received any of your letters. I never would've let a year's worth of them pile up without a reply. Passive-aggression is not my style."

He raised a hand, brushed a stray hair from her face, and tucked it behind her ear, his finger lingering a second before he removed it. "In hindsight, I understand that. But at the time, your silence crushed me. I was young and my pride was stung. By the time my contract with the army was up, I had decided to leave you alone and start over."

She nodded and felt something she hadn't wanted to do with this male in a long time—she wanted to tease him. She clicked her tongue. "Male shifters and their pride..."

He growled, and then tickled her side before she could move out of the way. She giggled against her will. "Stop it."

He stopped and captured one of her hands in his. "I need to know, Kaya. Do you forgive me for being an idiot and abandoning you, literally, to a pack of wolves at our mating engagement ceremony?"

~~~

Sy held his breath as he waited for Kaya to answer. This was about more than being able to date her or fuck her again. If she forgave him, it could be the beginning of a future he'd long given up. One of having a mate and maybe even cubs, and having someone he could stand beside as an equal, but also take care of.

Even if she said yes, nothing was guaranteed, but just the chance of reclaiming Kaya as his own was good enough for now.

Kaya squeezed his hand and said, "Yes. I forgive you."

He would focus one-hundred-and-ten percent on Markgen, but only after he kissed her.

Sy leaned over, raised his hand to her face, and lowered his lips to hers. After a long, lingering kiss, he pulled away to see a smile on Kaya's face. He smiled in return. "I couldn't help it. I had to kiss you."

"I know." She put a hand on his cheek and caressed his skin with her thumb. His inner cougar purred. "But the conversation about what any of this means will have to wait. Let's go upstairs. I'll tell you more about Markgen and we can come up with a plan."

"We? The fierce alpha wolf is going to allow the kitty cat to help her?"

She smiled. "Well, your nine lives will come in handy, if nothing else."

He grinned, kissed her one more time, and then unlocked the doors. "I think I have six of them left, and if you play your cards right, I might just give one or two of them to you."

Kaya shook her head and he slipped out of the car. As they made their way to the elevator, he placed a hand on the small of her back. With the heat of his wolf-shifter against his palm, something around his heart lightened.

With the possibility of this woman coming naked into his arms again, as well as her blossoming trust, Sy was happier than he'd been in a long time. He only hoped his luck would last.

CHAPTER NINE

When Kaya finished telling Sy the ins and outs of GreyFire's relationship with Markgen, she said, "While you could try to find someone to help us sneak inside their research facility, that would take precious time to put together and I believe there is an easier way to get information. I could set up a meeting to tour and inspect the facility. That way I could park a car in their lot with the necessary equipment and personnel to try and hack into their wireless network for information. If whoever sent the pup wasn't bright enough to cover their tracks on the flash drive, then they probably won't suspect shifters are smart enough to try and hack their emails or personal files."

Sy leaned back in his chair. "Wouldn't scheduling a meeting seem suspicious, though? That all of the sudden you want to visit this company you haven't visited in years. If the person who designed the unnamed virus is there, it will set off all kinds of red flags."

She shook her head. "Not really. I've been talking about a visit for months now. I need to meet the doctor in charge of the clinical trials and one of his superiors to finalize the profit percentages for each party, in case we get FDA approval. I think tiptoeing around Markgen will cause a bigger red flag than carrying on with business as usual."

"You mentioned having someone in the car to hack their network, which I assume you'll need my help to obtain, but would you be going inside the facility alone?"

"Yes to needing your help for a hacker, but no to going alone. I would need to bring some of GreyFire's researchers to help with the negotiations." He opened his mouth and she cut him off. "Having a cougar-shifter there would bring up too many questions. You know that."

Sy fell silent and Kaya tried not to hold her breath. The glint of shifter alpha male protectiveness was there in his eyes. How he handled this situation would tell her if he could handle her position as clan leader.

Sy finally said, "I know I can't go, and that kills me, but I trust you. If you think you can handle it, I believe you. All I ask is to have a contingency plan in case the virus is being stored there and you're exposed."

A sense of relief filled her at his answer and she nodded. "Of course." Kaya was about to lay out her plans when her cell phone rang and she answered, "Hello?"

"Kaya, it's Erika. We have a situation. While the infected pup was transferred successfully last night to our quarantine lab, the pup is now missing. We think someone broke into the lab and stole her."

Kaya frowned. "What?"

"No one knows who did it. Some of the sentries swept the area for evidence, but nothing unusual came up. I know you left me in charge, but this is big. What do you want me to do?"

Shit. Any of the wolves who came into contact with the pup could be infected. The virus was airborne as long as the infected wolf was still alive.

But she couldn't form a plan without more information. "How long has the pup been missing?"

"The last observation was two hours ago."

"Are any of the clan vehicles missing?"

"No. Jonathan has been trying to track the pup and mysterious thief, but whoever it was, they're good. He hasn't been able to determine if they're still inside the den or if they're out in the forest. I have someone talking with Kian right now to see if DarkStalker can help us. But Kaya, what should I do? The logical choice is to impose quarantine, but if the thief is still in the den, it'll let them know we've discovered the theft, which will give them time to hide. If the person is in the woods and we ban anyone from leaving the den, we wouldn't be able to go after them unless Kian's people helped."

Neither of the choices were ideal, but Kaya still didn't have enough information. "I'm going to call Kian right now and then call you back. While I do that, don't alert anyone to the situation who doesn't need to know."

Kaya clicked off her phone and turned to Sy. "Did you catch the conversation?"

He nodded. "Even in human form, my hearing is pretty good. I'm sure Kian will help, but if you want me to talk to him, I can."

"That would be easier, but if I want to ensure this alliance will work, I need to do it." She scrolled through her contacts. "But if you can come up with a few ideas of how to flush out the thief, I'll be happy to hear them when I'm done."

Sy nodded and Kaya put the phone to her ear. Kian picked up on the second ring. "Kaya?"

"Kian." She filled in the holes of what he didn't know and said, "I know the decision to try to make this alliance more than something written on paper happened only days ago, but I need your help. The best way to contain all of this is to quarantine GreyFire's den. The researchers there will continue to work on a cure, but I need to stay here and work on finding the source, just in case they can't come up with anything. However, I can only do this if you're willing to search the woods to look for the thief, just in case he or she escaped."

The line was silent for a second before Kian said, "I will, but only on two conditions."

She hadn't expected anything less. "What conditions?"

"When all of this is over and your clan is safe and virus-free, I want us to sit down and pen out a closer alliance treaty."

So far, so good. "And the other condition?"

"We're also going to hold a gathering of both of our clans before the winter snow sets in."

That was going to be harder to pull off. "Yes to the first condition, and I'll try my best for the second. While I can get my people to attend the gathering, I can't guarantee they'll enjoy it or not try to provoke fights with some of your cougars."

She could hear the amusement in Kian's voice. "I expect my people to act about the same, but a fight or two might actually bring them closer together."

She decided not to question his male logic right now. "So, does this mean you're going to help?"

"Yes. Give me twenty minutes to organize teams, and then start your quarantine. Also, if there are any of your sentries who are out on duty and need anything while they're stuck living in the small sentry shelters, they just have to ask."

It didn't surprise Kaya that Kian knew the logistics of her perimeter guard. "I really appreciate this, Kian."

"No worries. Just take care of my brother and try to find the source, and hopefully, the cure."

Before she could answer, the line went dead.

Rather than focus on that comment, she called Erika and explained the situation. With everything in place on her land, she turned off the phone and turned toward Sylas.

~~~

Sy watched and listened as Kaya calmly set things up with his brother and laid out a plan. Even with a pending disaster, she was quick-witted and cool under pressure. She deserved to be clan leader.

But he forced his mind to focus. Kaya had asked for ideas, and he needed to prove he could be of use to her.

He kept one ear on her conversations to keep track of the new information while he went through the possibilities of how the thief had broken in. Then something hit him, something that Kaya had overlooked.

He waited until she finished talking with her second-in-command. When she turned toward him, he said without preamble, "What if the thief didn't steal the pup for malicious purposes? Every clan has a soft heart or three who takes in the strays. Could one of your wolves have heard about the pup and found a way to get it out?"

"It's possible, but wolves as a whole are softhearted when it comes to pups. It's nearly impossible to pin it down to one or two people."

He nodded toward her phone. "Give Erika a list to check out, and not just the softhearted ones, but also for any parents who have recently lost a child."

He waited to see if she'd question his suggestion, but she merely nodded. "Okay, I'll talk with Erika about that. I also need to find out which researchers are clear of the den to join me in a meeting with Markgen, as well as organize my sentries currently on guard." She paused and he raised an eyebrow in question. She sighed. "I hate to ask you this, as you're much more than an errand boy, but if I'm going to make it through all of this without fainting, I could use some coffee and something to eat. Could you help me out and get something for me? I don't care what, as long as it's edible."

He could see how asking him to do this was difficult, but just the fact she'd asked him at all seemed important. Sy didn't think she asked for help often enough.

He stood up, walked over to her, and framed her lovely, bronze face with his hands. At his touch, her breath hitched and he wished he could act on it. Instead, he said, "Never be afraid to ask me for help, Kaya." He caressed her cheeks with his thumbs. "Although, I may ask for a few favors along the way."

She frowned. "Favors? I had expected better of you, Sylas—"

He shut her up with a kiss, sucking her bottom lip between his and biting gently. Then he slipped his tongue inside her mouth and tangled with hers for a few seconds before he retreated and said, "I think you'll like the favors I want to ask for in return. Consider your kiss a down payment." He gave her one more quick kiss. "I'll get you some food and coffee, and later you can let me devour you until I've had my fill."

Color flushed her cheeks. "Sy."

He grinned and released her. "I'll take that as yes, you'll let me. Now, do what you need to do to save your clan. I have my cell if something comes up, but I'll be back soon."

She reached out and grabbed his hand. "Wait, before you go. Do you think Dave would help us, or at least know someone trustworthy who could?"

"For hacking into Markgen's network?" Kaya nodded and he continued. "Maybe. When you call him, try mentioning my name and the word 'burning dawn'."

She gave him a wry look. "You have a secret code phrase? Seriously?"

Sy shrugged. "It works. He'll still call me to double-check, but the phrase will make him more apt to believe you."

She released his hand. "Okay, fine. Can you give me his number?" After he rattled off Dave's number, she smiled up at him. "Thanks, Sy."

He cupped her cheek, and then ran his hand to the back of her neck and squeezed. "Anything else?"

She shook her head. "No. Just be careful. Whoever is behind this is probably watching us."

"No worries. I'm always careful, Kaya-love."

She smiled at the old endearment. With herculean effort, he released his grip and she started dialing. As he went to grab his wallet, Sy couldn't stop smiling. Even in private, Kaya was letting him touch her at will. If that wasn't a good enough sign, she had also asked for his help. If they could just get this damn assignment over with, he could start figuring out a way to win her over for good.

For now, he would have to settle with doing errands and supporting her however he could to prove how serious he was about wanting her. Hopefully, with time, she'd trust him with much more.

Smiling at that thought, he went out the door and headed down the stairs.

Reclaiming the Wolf

~~~

A few hours later, Kaya clicked off her cell phone, laid it on the table, and stretched her arms over her head. Her ear was warm from being on her phone for so long, but everything was in place. The quarantine was set, and Kian's people were deployed. Dave had also responded to Sy's cheesy pass-phrase and said he would check in with Sy about hacking into Markgen's network. And finally, her meeting was schedule with Markgen for tomorrow morning.

Once she finished stretching, she looked over to see Sy doing something on his laptop on the couch, much like he'd been doing since he'd come back with food and coffee. Before she could say anything, he shut the laptop, looked at her, and said, "All done?"

"Yes, finally. Erika and Kian will keep me updated, but both want me to focus on tomorrow's meeting."

"Do you have a lot left to do?"

"Yes and no. My researchers will email me some information to look over later tonight. They should arrive in Seattle early tomorrow morning, and we'll go over both the proposal and what to do if things turn south before the meeting."

"Good." Sy patted the spot on the couch next to him. "Come here."

She looked at him with suspicion. "Care to tell me what for?"

"Can't a man have some surprises? Just come here, Kaya."

"A surprise?"

He answered by just patting the couch again.

"Okay." She got up and went over to the couch. As soon as she sat down, Sy hauled her up onto his lap. "Sylas, what are you doing? Just because my phone calls are finished doesn't mean I have free time to fool around."

His squeezed her hip. "I think you need to go for a run."

She blinked at the change of topic. "I can't, Sylas. What if Kian and Erika need me? The last I heard, they don't make cell phone carrying cases or earpieces for wolves."

"You're wrong. But before I show you the surprise I bought when I was out, you owe me a kiss for doing your errands." She opened her mouth and he placed a hand over her lips, the warmth of his fingers reminding her of what else those talented fingers could do. He continued, "I admire your strength and determination in taking care of your clan, but, Kaya, you have enough time to unwind a little. I have a feeling you're cooped up inside your office most of the time and it's probably driving your wolf crazy." He slid his fingers from her lips to her chin. "Let her out for a bit tonight. I can hold the fort."

As she stared into his green eyes ringed with gold, her inner wolf wanted to lick him in gratitude for the suggestion. It seemed her wolf had sided against Kaya this time. Not that she could tell Sy that, or she'd never hear the end of it. "One kiss?"

He waggled his eyebrows. "Unless you ask for more, of course."

She smiled at his silly actions and raised a hand to his cheek. Since he'd shaved earlier, his skin was now smooth with a touch of roughness. As she rubbed her thumb on his cheek, she missed the feel of his short whiskers. Without thinking, she said, "I miss your scruff."

He grinned and captured her hand against his cheek. "Why, because of the way it feels against your inner thigh? Or against the sensitive skin of your pussy lips?"

Rather than try to avoid his question, she decided to be honest. "Both."

He growled before he raised his head and nipped her bottom lip. "Kiss me, Kaya, and make it good."

Rather than scold him for ordering her around, she raised a finger to his mouth. She traced his bottom lip, and then the top one, before pushing her finger between them. He never broke eye contact as he sucked her finger deep and caressed her skin with his tongue. The combination of the pull of his mouth and tickling of his tongue made her instantly wet.

His nostrils flared, but he never stopped sucking her finger. He was waiting for her to kiss him.

She removed her finger and ran her hand around his neck and into his hair. She leaned down and simply took a second to stare into Sy's hot, intense gaze. Everything about his eyes said he wanted her.

And right now, she wanted him too.

She took his mouth in a kiss, taking her time to explore his lips, his teeth, and his tongue. As she took the kiss deeper, he never moved anything apart from his tongue. Frustrated, she pulled away and said, "Why aren't you touching me, Sylas?"

"Because you never said I could."

"Touch me, Sy. I've gone too many years without this kind of closeness. I want you to touch me."

He moved a hand from her hip to the hem of her shirt. She gave him a look and said, "But no tickling."

He smiled, but the heat never faded from his eyes. "We can negotiate that point later."

Then his hand was under her shirt. He laid his palm on her ribcage, and the heat of his touch shot straight between her legs. As he stroked her skin, her pussy started to throb in time with his movements. When he stilled his hand, she growled. "Don't stop."

"Oh, I don't intend on stopping."

He moved his hand to the waistband of her jeans and undid the button. As he slowly slid down the zipper, her heart rate kicked up. She wanted to feel his rough fingers against the swollen, sensitive skin between her thighs.

He placed his hand under the top of her underwear and slowly moved his hand down until it rested just above her clit. His voice was husky when he said, "Are you wet enough to take my cock?"

She let out a breathy, "Yes."

His gaze heated. "Let's find out."

But he didn't move his hand. He simply stared into her eyes and nipped her chin. She opened her mouth to tell him to get a move on, but before she could say a word, he thrust a finger between her folds.

She tightened her grip on his hair at the sudden intrusion. "Sy."

As he rubbed his finger up and down her slit, Kaya gripped his shoulder for support with her free hand. She felt the vibration of his chuckle before he said, "Yes, you're fucking drenched for me." He pressed against her clit and she cried out. "You're still going for a run, Kaya-love, but let me fuck you first." He started to move a finger inside her pussy and she let out a moan. "You know you want to feel how deep my cock can be while you ride me," he stilled his finger and she let out a noise of frustration, which only made Sy smile at her, "and how well I can fill that empty ache between your thighs." He removed his finger. "So, what's it going to be?"

She was so swollen and aching that there was only one answer. "Fuck me, Sy."

"And then you'll go for a run?"

"Yes, then a run."

He smiled and removed his hand from her pants. "Okay, now stand up and strip."

CHAPTER TEN

Kaya slid off Sy's lap and he palmed his cock through his jeans. He hadn't planned to fuck Kaya before her run. But when she hadn't tried to move from his lap and then proceeded to seduce him with her slow, deliberate movements of her fingers on his lips before pushing one of her digits into his mouth, getting his cock inside her was all he could think about.

As the sexiest women he'd ever known removed her shirt and then her bra to bare her smooth, tanned skin and dark nipples, he undid his jeans and shimmied out of them. While she slid her jeans down her long legs, he tore off his shirt. Since he was now naked, he took his dick in hand and stroked it as Kaya removed her underwear to reveal the neatly-trimmed, dark hair between her legs.

She looked up at him and then down at his hand; his cock pulsed under her scrutiny. She licked her lips, causing a drop of precum to leak out. He hoped like hell licking her lips was a signal she was going to suck his dick deep into that luscious mouth of hers.

Without a word, she kneeled on the floor between his thighs and pushed his legs wider. Sy stilled his hand as she traced his knuckles, her touch feather light and warm. The fantasy he'd had earlier, about him fucking Kaya's mouth, might just come true.

RECLAIMING THE WOLF

He stopped breathing as she gently lifted each of his digits up off his cock, and when he finally let go, his cock curled heavy and hard against his belly. Kaya took his wrist, lifted his hand, and kissed his palm. He groaned when she flicked her wet tongue against his skin, forcing out a few more drops of precum. His voice was husky when he whispered, "Kaya."

At his voice she looked up and smiled at him. This wasn't the teenager who'd been shy and embarrassed about sucking his cock. Kaya was a woman who understood the power she held over him.

And damn, she was sexy.

Without breaking eye contact, she took his cock in her other hand, her palm warm and soft. All he could think about was how he wanted to feel her mouth around his dick, twirling and sucking, until he could brand her mouth with his seed and his scent.

Yes, his cougar liked that idea. Branding the female. She was theirs.

Kaya swept her hair over one shoulder, and the long, thick strands tickled his thigh. He wanted to thread his fingers into her hair and fist it, but he wanted to wait and see what she would do first. He was allowing her to be in control. For now.

She leaned down until one of her hard nipples brushed his thigh, her lips now a mere inch from the head of his dick. He could feel her hot breath on his sensitive skin and it took everything he had not to push her sweet mouth down.

Thankfully, he didn't have to wait long.

Kaya licked the tip with her hot little tongue, one stroke and then another, until she'd cleaned every drop of precum off. Then she blew on his cock, and Sy groaned, "Kaya, you're killing me, love."

107

With a wicked glint in her eyes, she took his cock deep into her mouth and swallowed. He could feel the back of her throat. He grabbed her head so she wouldn't move away and leave him panting for more like a goddamn teenager.

Sensing she was about to reach her limit, he reluctantly let go and she retreated, but she quickly took him deep again and started to move.

Fuck. The warmth of her mouth as she moved up and down was better than he remembered. As she swirled and traced his cock with her tongue, it took everything not to come right then and there. That became all the harder when she started to massage and squeeze his balls.

Damn, she gave good head. He'd reward her later with his tongue.

Despite his best efforts to last a little longer, Sy felt the pressure at the base of his spine, which signaled he was about to come. As much as both he and his cougar wanted to brand her mouth with his hot seed, he didn't have time to come both in her mouth and in her pussy, and right now, he wanted her pussy more. He growled and said, "Kaya, stop."

She released his cock, but gave the head one last swipe with her tongue before she looked up. Her brown eyes were heavy with desire, and as her tongue peeked out to catch a drop of spit from the corner of her mouth, he was at his limit. "Vixen. As much as I love the caresses of your hot mouth on my cock, I want to feel your tight little pussy as you ride my dick and take it deep inside you." He brushed her cheek with his finger. "Now, come here."

With a sexy smile, she ran her hands up his thighs, over his stomach, and grabbed onto his shoulders as she stood up. She straddled his body, resting her legs on the couch cushions on either side of him. He tried to kiss her, but she moved her head and shook it. "Not yet."

Curious to see what she'd do, he waited. Her hand slid down his chest and gripped his cock. She squeezed and he instinctively thrust into her hand. Then the head of his cock was at her wet pussy. He was tempted to thrust, but before he could, Kaya sank down, taking him to the hilt.

The way her hot, wet sheath fit around his cock was perfect—a little tight, but with just the right amount of pressure.

She placed her hands on his chest, but didn't move her lower body. Instead, she stared into his eyes and said, "I've missed this."

The tenderness of her voice sparked something inside him. He'd tried so hard to forget Kaya and move on, but now he couldn't remember why. This wolf-shifter female was his—now and forever.

He just needed to make sure she understood that.

He would wait to share his claim for when they had more time. For now, he pulled her head to his and kissed her in return. What he couldn't say with words, he conveyed with his mouth, his tongue, and his teeth.

He ran his hands down her smooth, toned back until he palmed her round ass cheeks. He broke the kiss and said, "I've missed this too, Kaya-love. Now, ride me like there's no tomorrow."

~~~

At Sy's old endearment, her heart softened a little. The sex back in the cave had been just that—sex. But now, with the teasing and the endearments and Sy helping her with her tasks, she was starting to believe this was something more.

Rather than take him hard and fast, Kaya moved her hips in slow, deliberate movements, knowing it would drive Sy crazy.

As she rode up and down her cougar-shifter's cock, she reached out a hand to touch his face, a face that was both familiar and different from the last time she'd rode this male. Would this be the last time she'd see his vulnerable expression as he came?

A few days ago, she'd never have imagined she'd be here again with Sylas Murray, let alone be fucking him on a couch. But the more time they spent together, the more she realized how much she'd missed him.

Of course, he might soon get fed up with her and leave all over again. It wasn't like she had a claim on him.

Her wolf growled at the thought of losing him, but Kaya pushed her inner animal back. She couldn't force Sy to stay with her. Hell, probably few people could force Sy to do anything. But once all of this damn looking and searching for a cure was done, she could see what happened.

Then Sy's warm, rough hands caressed her back and she focused back on him as he said, "Why the frown, Kaya? Is it really that bad?"

"I'm not frowning."

"You are."

Shit. She'd let down her guard without realizing it.

Rather than think about what that meant, she picked up her pace and leaned close to his lips. "Am I frowning now?"

He groaned as she twirled her hips in a circle. He finally hissed, "I don't fucking care. Just give me more of that."

She complied, loving the way his cock reached deep inside her pussy. For good measure, she dug her claws into Sy's chest.

As if knowing what she needed, he gripped her ass hard and started moving her hips faster.

As the sound of their flesh meeting filled the room, she cried out when his cock finally hit her g-spot. "Yes, right there."

Growling, Sy gripped her ass even harder, to the point his nails were digging into her cheeks.

Fuck, she'd missed sex like this.

Without having to ask, one of his hands released her ass and slipped between their bodies to rub her clit. At his rough, quick brushes of his fingers, Kaya whispered, "Sylas."

At his heated gaze and smug smile, Kaya's heart skipped a beat. She was in trouble.

He rubbed even faster and it took everything she had to keep her eyes open; she wanted to see Sy's face when he came.

The pressure started to build and with a few more firm strokes of her clit, pleasure shot through her body.

Her cougar continued to move her up and down his cock until he tensed and cried out. Maybe she was imagining things, but she swore she could feel each jet of his hot, wet semen inside her.

As he came down from his orgasm, Sy moved his hands to caress her sides, then her neck, until they finally rest on her cheeks. He brought her head down for a gentle, lingering kiss before he pressed her head to his shoulder.

Afraid words would break the spell, Kaya simply laid against his chest, breathing in the scent of sex, male, and cougar. Right here, right now, she wasn't a leader responsible for hundreds of people; she was just a woman lying against the chest of a man she'd once loved.

As Sy's hand started to caress her back, she nuzzled deeper against him, loving the combined feel of his cock inside her and his chest pressed against hers. While her wolf had been anxious to come out for a run, it was content to simply lie against the cougar-shifter for a little while. He made the human half of her feel warm and protected, and the wolf approved.

Sy's hand stopped caressing her, but only to wrap his arms around her and hug her tight. He kissed the top of her head and said, "Do you want to see your present now?"

She wanted to scream, "No!" and simply lie against his chest all night. Maybe even sleep in his arms, but it was too soon for her to make any claim on him. While his body obviously wanted her, she wasn't quite sure about his heart.

Kaya brushed her hand through the hair on his chest and forced herself to not act as if the sex had been anything more mutual orgasms. Keeping her voice light, she said, "As long as it's not a dog muzzle, then I suppose so."

She loved hearing the rumble inside his chest as he laughed. "No, as much as it'd be handy to have, it's not a muzzle." He lightly tapped her ass. "But in order for me to get it, you need to get up. Strong as I am, I don't think I can manage to keep us joined as I stand up, walk across the room, and search through my bag."

Smiling, she pushed up until she could meet his eyes. "What, you're not invincible anymore? I seem to remember a teenage boy telling me he could do anything as long as he got a little creative."

Sy grinned and the sight warmed her heart. "That teenage boy was a dumbass. It took him a long time to realize it."

She laughed. "Good to see the man version of him can admit it."

She moved to stand up but Sy kept his arms wrapped around her. "How about a kiss as a reward?"

"For telling me what I already knew?"

"Is that a no? Then in that case..."

He tickled her sides and Kaya couldn't stop laughing. "Stop it...Sylas..."

He stopped and took her lips in a rough, possessive kiss. When he pulled away, he lightly slapped her ass again and released his hold on her. "Stand up before I change my mind and keep you in my lap all night long."

She almost said that was what she wanted too, but she'd been hurt once before by this male and she didn't want it to happen again. Until she was sure of Sy's intentions and ability to withstand the scrutiny of a cross-species pairing, she would keep her deepest growing desire—for Sylas to be her mate, to help with her loneliness, and to always stand by her side—to herself.

She stood up and placed her hands on her hips. "Okay, so where's my present?"

~~~

Missing Kaya's weight and heat on his lap, Sy wanted nothing more than to go over and haul her back, but he wasn't about to be selfish. As a teenager, he had always taken what he wanted and never really considered Kaya's needs until she had mentioned them. If he was to ever show he was worthy of being her mate, then he needed to show her how he'd really changed.

He'd made a good start with supporting her earlier by doing her errands, but it wasn't enough. He needed her to be able to trust him with her heart. One way to do that was to please her wolf and get it on his side.

Ignoring his cock's desire to toss Kaya down and fuck her again, he moved across the room and took out a small paper bag from his satchel. He held it out. "Here."

She walked over and took the bag. Looking inside, she frowned. "Is this a dog collar?"

"Yes, but look under the collar."

She darted a "look" at him before reaching into the bag and pulling out the cell phone placed inside a belt clip.

Sy said, "If we set the phone to vibrate, attached the heavy-duty clip to the collar, and then put the collar around your neck in wolf form, you'll always know when someone's trying to get a hold of you. Then it's just a matter of shifting, removing the collar, and making the call. I already took the liberty of informing Erika, Kian, and some of the others about the new number to call if you don't answer your usual cell number."

She stared at the collar and phone in her hands, and he started to wonder if he'd done something wrong. "Kaya? You don't have to wear it if you don't want to. It was just a spur of the moment idea so I could run with you, but I can stay human and handle the calls while you run, if you'd rather do that."

Kaya rushed over to him and wrapped her arms around his waist. "No, no, it's thoughtful of you, Sy. It's so simple, but it never would've crossed my mind to do something like this."

He hugged her tight against his body, loving the way she fit against him. "Oh, I think I know how you can thank me later."

She looked up. "Sylas."

He grinned and she smiled back at him. He was tempted to tease her some more, but he glanced at the clock on the far wall and noticed the time. "If you want to go for a run, Kaya, we need to leave. Go clean-up and be ready in five minutes."

She gave him a squeeze. "Yes, sir."

Reclaiming the Wolf

She released her hold and headed for the bedroom. He watched her tight, round ass until it disappeared behind the bathroom door.

Now that Kaya had accepted his gift, his cougar was anxious to come out to play too. His cat remembered what it'd been like before and was more than ready to tangle with the wolf, like in the old days, and see what new tricks she had up her sleeve.

~~~

In wolf form, Kaya waited patiently as Sy secured the collar-slash-phone contraption around her neck. The instant he was done, she ran to the side of the clearing and then sniffed the bushes and flowers around the edges to see what she could find.

She'd missed the chance to be outside and do something as simple as run in her wolf form. She wasn't a cat shifter, but if she had been, she'd be purring right about now.

Sy was still squatting on his haunches in human form with a smile on his face as he watched her dart around. Running back over to him, she licked his face in gratitude for bringing her here to a shifter-designated forest across the lake from Seattle. He laughed, and then scratched her jaw with one hand and behind her ear with the other. Since it was just Sy here with her, she let her tongue loll out in contentment.

He dropped his hands to pat her sides and said, "Now, go for a run, Kaya-love. We should probably head back in about an hour to make sure you have enough time to go over your researchers' files and get some sleep before your meeting in the morning."

She looked at him and let out a yip. When he shook his head and said, "I don't speak wolf," she grabbed the hem of his shirt with her teeth and tugged, hoping he'd understand what she wanted.

He pet her head and said, "Do you want the cougar to come out to play?" She barked again, and he stood up. "Okay, but just don't expect me to behave like one of your wolves. Us cats like to be sneaky rather than confrontational."

She gave a low growl and he laughed. "Okay, okay. I'll admit that some cats can be confrontational."

He tugged off his shirt and she sat down on her haunches. She wanted to watch him shift.

Once Sy stood unabashedly naked under the moon, he closed his eyes in concentration, which was a display of trust she didn't miss.

His body started to change shape as his arms elongated into paws, his head morphed into a feline head with large teeth, and a long, tan tail grew out of his backside. Within seconds, a large male cougar with a tan coat, green eyes, and a pink nose covered in dark spots stood in front of her. He let out a "cougar-chirp" that sounded like a big cat's meow and she charged at him, anxious to play.

She managed to tumble him to the ground, but he outweighed her and easily regained the upper hand. He'd nearly pinned her to the ground when she escaped and darted to the far side of the clearing. She barked and took off into the woods.

As Sy chased her, Kaya felt some of the weight she'd been carrying on her shoulders disappear. To be able to run in her wolf-form was a special kind of joy that she'd been denying too much as of late.

There might be a possible threat to her clan, but thanks to Sy and his little contraption around her neck, she was able to take a brief break to unwind and get her mind ready for tomorrow.

And she could do it all while still being available to her clan if they needed her.

Erika had tried hard to take care of her over the last three years since Kaya had become clan leader, but Kaya had still outranked her. Erika could never truly make her do anything, but Sylas Murray was outside her pack structure, and he damn well knew it. He wasn't afraid to push her to do something she would've brushed aside as unimportant, such as letting her wolf free, when in reality, it was extremely important to her mental health and her ability to face tough situations.

As they chased and tumbled over the next hour, playing the most juvenile of shifter games, Kaya was happier than she'd been in a long time. If things went well tomorrow at Markgen, and her clan was protected, she decided to risk her heart again with Sy and see what happened.

She'd never met anyone like him, and she doubted she'd ever do so again.

Chapter Eleven

The next morning, Sy stretched out his muscles in his cougar form. First he reached out with his front paws and extended his claws. Then he half stood to stretch his hind legs and claws. After a long yawn, he blinked his eyes and jumped down from his bed to check on Kaya. He'd very nearly curled up against her back in his cougar form, but he had finally decided not to so she could get some sleep. If he had entered her bedroom and lain on her bed, the temptation to shift back into a man and take her again, this time to savor every inch of her body, would've been too great.

As a shifter male, his restraint only went so far.

He stopped to peek into Kaya's room, but it was empty. Since he didn't hear any sounds coming from her attached bathroom, he went to the kitchen. It was also empty, but the smell of brewed coffee told him Kaya had been here already. He spotted the message scribbled on the white board on the fridge. *I left early. I'll call you when I'm done with my meeting.*

He knew Kaya had a job to do, but he felt a little pang of disappointment at knowing she'd already gone.

Still, she had an entire clan's future riding on her back and she couldn't always do what she wanted. After working for years with his brother, Kian, he knew that better than most.

RECLAIMING THE WOLF

Sy gave one last cat stretch before he imagined his paws becoming arms, his teeth receding, and his tail merging back into his spine. The familiar flash of pleasure and pain coursed through his body before he was human again.

After pouring his coffee, he booted up his laptop. He had some clan stuff to do before his visit with DS Engineering's branch office later today, but he had fifteen or twenty minutes to work on his surprise for Kaya.

Just as he opened up his document on his computer, his cell phone rang. He reached across the table, glanced at the screen to see it was Erika from GreyFire and tapped the receive button. "Yes?"

"Kaya's in her meeting, isn't she?"

"She's not here and she left a note saying she was going to it. Why?"

"I can't get a hold of her, and I really need to."

Sy didn't like the desperation in Erika's voice. While he was technically an outsider, he decided to ask, "What's wrong?"

She paused, and he thought she wasn't going to answer, but then she let out a breath and said, "I don't think I should tell you, but since Kaya told me to call you if I can't get a hold of her this morning, I have no choice."

He'd think about the importance of that statement later. For now, he fell back on his training in both the army and as his brother's second. He steeled his voice and said, "Then tell me."

She huffed a little into the phone, but he knew she'd give in rather than disobey her clan leader. "Several of our clan members have started showing symptoms similar to the infected wolf-shifters."

"How many?"

"Five so far, but it won't be long before their families and friends start displaying the same symptoms since the virus is airborne in living wolf-shifters."

"Did you find any connections between the five infected shifters?"

"Yes. They all work as cleaners for the research labs. If that wasn't enough, they haven't seen one of their co-workers since the infected wolf pup disappeared. The woman's name is Jenna and she recently lost her pup to an accident. If she decided to use this new one to replace it, she's probably already attached and would most likely forfeit her life before giving up the infected child."

Just as he'd suggested earlier. "Okay, so we have a suspect, which is great, but what about a cure? Have your researchers been able to use the cougar-shifter blood to concoct something?"

"I hadn't gotten that far yet. But yes, they've narrowed down some of the cougar-shifter antibodies that offer protection against the virus. This morning a test on some samples was promising, but not yet definitive. It could be weeks before they have something they can be sure will kill or protect against the virus."

They didn't have weeks.

But then Sy had an idea. "Medical research is not my strong point, so shoot me down if need be, but what about transfusing a cougar-shifter's blood into one of the wolves? Would that offer the necessary protection since none of the cougar-shifters have shown symptoms despite direct contact with the infected?"

"Giving a wolf-shifter cougar blood is risky. From past experiments, we know it could kill them."

"Well, all of the infected will die anyway. You should at least give them the option."

The line went silent again. He hated having conversations over the phone. At least face-to-face he could read facial cues and body language. His inner cougar wanted to assess where Erika was on the dominance scale so the cat could plan his attack.

Thankfully, Erika's voice came back on the line before he snapped at her. "Fine. I have no idea if it'll work or not, but I'll consult with some of our specialists and if they think it may have a positive effect, then we'll give the infected people the option."

"Good. Does my brother know about the pup's disappearance?"

Erika sounded irritated when she replied. "Of course he does. Look, I'm only talking with you because Kaya said I had to do it. You really don't have any sway over what happens within GreyFire, so stop pretending you do."

His instincts told him she wasn't telling the whole truth. "What did Kaya say exactly? And don't lie, as you know as well as I do that she won't tolerate it."

Erika growled. "Cougar, you're pushing my limits."

"Just tell me, wolf."

"Fine. She declared a temporary power share with you."

Sy blinked, not expecting that answer. When a clan leader declared a power share it meant the person they shared it with could make decisions on behalf of the clan if they became incapacitated.

Frankly, he couldn't believe Kaya had done it since it was a tremendous responsibility. The fact she had, told him volumes about how she was starting to see him.

Although, truth be told, Sy had a small niggling that she'd done it to ensure the truce between GreyFire and DarkStalker would continue to grow closer in the future. Not everyone shared

Kaya's vision on the three shifter clans of the Cascade Mountains working together.

Of course, he doubted he'd ever need to use the power share to take charge. Kaya would be back later today.

He said, "Okay, then. For now, you're right; you don't have to listen to me. But you do have to keep me in the loop until Kaya checks in. If anything—anything at all—happens, let me know."

There was a pause before Erika said, "You're sleeping with her again, aren't you?"

His inner cougar growled. "That is Kaya's business and has nothing to do with the situation in your clan. Go talk with your specialists about the cougar-shifter blood transfusions before the infected get any sicker."

He clicked off his phone before Erika could argue any further. He doubted if he was a wolf-shifter she would've held the same reservations about Kaya declaring a power share with him. And right now, he didn't have time for that species-bias bullshit.

He glanced at the clock on his computer. Damn, the call with Erika had taken up his free time. If he was going to make his eleven a.m. appointment, he needed to start getting ready.

Sy headed for his room. If the blood transfusions worked, that would buy both the GreyFire researchers and Kaya some time.

He really hoped Dave succeeded in hacking into Markgen's network and discovering something that would lead them to a cure. True, finding incriminating evidence might lead to Kaya sneaking into Markgen and putting her life in danger, but he knew he couldn't stop her. One of the reasons he cared for Kaya was because of her take-charge attitude and her ability to follow through.

Reclaiming the Wolf

He really hoped she asked for his help. He wanted to
support her, but he couldn't be a submissive male who did
whatever she asked. He wanted to be able to act on something
without forever checking in with her. A break-in to Markgen
might force him to share that fact sooner rather than later.

But he only wanted to help Kaya because if anything
happened to the GreyFire wolves, it would destroy the woman he
was starting to care for again and that thought made his cougar
snarl. Both Sy and his cat wanted her to be happy.

And they would do anything to make that happen, provided
they could do it together as a team.

~~~

Kaya sat inside Markgen's main building at a long
conference table inside one of the meeting rooms, her two
GreyFire researchers on either side of her. Security for the
parking lot and the main building had been much laxer than she'd
anticipated. Of course, that made her a little nervous. Anytime
something was too easy, there always seemed to be a catch.

While her inner wolf paced inside her head, Kaya kept up
her cool, collected mien; her black pantsuit and hair pulled into a
bun screamed business professional. Since too many people liked
to dismiss shifters as animals, over the years Kaya had learned
that a good suit and heels could unsettle a human just as much as
baring her teeth.

It also helped Kaya to maintain her composure since the
suit was like a costume for one of her many roles inside GreyFire.

She glanced to the clock on the far wall. Dr. Wesley Smith
was now thirty minutes late. Kaya understood the power of

keeping someone waiting, but it was starting to border on ridiculous.

Another ten minutes passed before a young woman in a gray skirt and pink top came into the room and said, "I'm sorry, but something has come up. Dr. Smith needs to reschedule the meeting for a different day."

Shit. Maybe someone had discovered Sy's contact hacking into their network and Markgen needed to implement some kind of security protocol. She had no way of knowing if that had happened or not, so she acted as if she were a little bored and irritated. "Did he say when?"

The woman shook her head. "No, but if you could call back tomorrow, we can try to reschedule."

She raised her eyebrows and tapped one of her forefingers on the table in front of her to display her irritation. "Dr. Smith does realize how important this meeting is, doesn't he? Besides, it's a three hour drive from my land to here. I can't just drop everything and come running."

Kaya could smell the woman's anxiety. The human swallowed before she said, "I'm just delivering his message. There's nothing I can do."

Kaya decided she'd put up enough of a fit to put off any suspicion that she was here for more than just a meeting. She stood up and her researchers followed suit. "Next time, Dr. Smith will have to come to GreyFire's land. You have my office number to set it all up."

The woman nodded and Kaya moved toward the door. The human jumped out of the way so the security guard on stand-by could escort them back to the entrance.

Ten minutes later, Kaya was inside the minivan they'd borrowed for the visit. One of her researchers was driving it, and soon they turned out onto the main road that led to the freeway. She tried calling Sy, but all she got was his voicemail. He must be doing his routine visit at DS Engineering.

She sent him a quick text message and instantly received a reply. *I'll be done in a few hours. Call Erika.*

Okay, that made her a little anxious.

Since she didn't want anyone in the car to overhear her conversation, Kaya reviewed Erika's emails, but they were vague. Obviously, her second didn't want to risk someone hacking her account. She'd just have to wait until she reached the safety of Sy's apartment to call her second. If it were a "call me this instant" type of situation, Erika would've given the emergency code word.

As the minivan sped down the freeway, she decided they were now far enough away from Markgen and it should be safe to question and see how Sy's contact Dave had done with hacking Markgen's network. She turned around in her seat and asked Dave, "How did it go?"

Dave looked up from his computer. "Their security was pretty lax and parts of it were probably done by a fresh college graduate. The company is even backing up their email over the cloud."

Kaya vaguely knew what he was talking about, but she wasn't afraid to ask for an explanation. "Explain why backing up to a cloud is important."

Dave nodded. "Well, the cloud is basically like sending your files over the internet to a virtual storage space. Just like with a physical storage space, if you don't have a good, strong lock, someone can break-in and steal all your stuff." He jerked his thumb behind them. "Whoever is in charge of Markgen's security hasn't put a very strong lock on some of their information. The proprietary documents were well guarded, but not their emails. I downloaded as much as I could, mainly from the last month or so, and saved them. If you and Sy sift through them, I'm sure you can find something."

Although she tried not to get her hopes up, she wanted him to be right.

Kaya took a good look at the human helping them and said, "While I appreciate all of your help, why are you willing to risk helping shifters? If you're caught breaking the law, sentences are twice as harsh if it's shifter-related."

Dave shrugged. "Sy saw my potential in the company and wasn't afraid to promote me despite my less than clean legal past. I owe him my second chance."

Yes, that sounded like Sylas. Taking well-calculated chances seemed to be his thing. He'd done the very same thing with her, after all.

Kaya nodded. "Well, you also have my thanks. You are welcome on GreyFire's land anytime, and if you ever need a favor, I can't promise anything, but I'll see what I can do."

Dave nodded. "I doubt I'll make it up to the mountains as I like it here, but thanks all the same." He removed something from his computer and held it out. She saw it was a flash drive. "I hope you find what you're looking for on here."

Kaya took the small, rectangular drive. "I hope so, too."

But as they drove back to the dummy location where they would switch cars before heading to Sy's apartment, Kaya had a feeling things had gone a little too smoothly. She only hoped this wasn't the calm before the storm.

Even if it were, she liked the fact she had Sy to help her if she needed it. She'd managed to lead GreyFire by herself over the last three years by sheer force of will, but she was starting to understand that if she ever wanted to achieve a balance between her duties and her happiness, she would need help. The only question was whether Sy would be that person or not.

Chapter Twelve

Sy unlocked the door to his apartment and entered to find Kaya sitting at the dining room table with his laptop. He'd given her the password last night, but now that he saw her using it, he wondered if she'd seen the surprise he was working on for her. He hoped not.

He'd received her text about news to share, so he came up behind her to see what she was working on, but it was just some emails. He placed his hands on her shoulders, squeezed, and said, "What's your news?"

"Dave managed to get two months' worth of Markgen's emails. I'm hoping to find something in them to help us."

He massaged her shoulders and he felt some of the tension ease out of her body. "Did you find anything yet?"

"No." She looked up with a frown and he stilled his fingers. "Did you really have to antagonize my second in command? Erika didn't like you before, and she definitely doesn't like you now."

He smiled. "But it's so fun."

"Sylas."

He stroked her cheek with one of his knuckles, but her expression didn't soften. So much for having a distracting touch. "Is there a reason I should start being nice to her? It's not like she visits DarkStalker's land every other weekend." When she didn't say anything, he decided to push. "I heard about the power share. Tell me what it means, Kaya."

Kaya closed the laptop with a sigh. "I guess I can take a short break."

She stood up and he put his hands on her hips to keep her from moving away. "Well?"

She stared into his eyes, but her expression was guarded. His cougar didn't like that. He wanted her to always be open with them.

Kaya said, "I want our clans to be closer, and I think you would make sure that happened if anything ever happened to me. I've started to trust you again, Sy. I'm not sure why, exactly, since we've only been working together again for a short time, but my wolf trusts you and I trust her."

The fact she just admitted her wolf trusted him made his cougar stretch out in his mind and purr because his cat trusted Kaya too.

But he knew, or at least hoped, there was more. "Is that the only reason, Kaya?"

She looked off to the side and said, "And, well, once all of this is over..."

He stroked her hips to ease her nervousness. Given their past, this conversation wasn't easy for either of them.

Once she finally looked back at him, he tilted his head and said, "Yes?"

"I want to try again, Sy. But this time, no hiding or sneaking around. I want it to be in full view of my clan. I don't have time to keep guessing if you want this or not, so just tell me straight."

As much as his cougar was growling in agreement and urging him to claim her, Sy wanted to be honest with her. "I can't be your errand boy, Kaya. If you want to try again, then it's as equals. Pulling rank will fall on deaf ears. I won't embarrass you in front of your clan, but I won't be just a shadow inside it either."

She smiled. "I don't want a servant; I want a partner."

Thank fuck. He pulled her up against his body. "That I can do."

He lowered his head to kiss her, but Kaya pushed against his chest. "Too much shit is going on in my clan. As much as I want to, I can't do this right now. Hot, mind-blowing sex will have to wait."

His ego pumped up a notch at her description of "mind-blowing," but to calm his cougar's need to scent-mark her, he kissed the tip of her nose and released her. "Then tell me what you've found and what needs doing. Erika sent me an update that the doctors are trying the cougar blood transfusions, but not if they're effective or not. Did they work?"

She patted his chest and moved back to sit in front of the laptop. "It's too soon to tell. But a few more wolves have fallen sick."

While he couldn't see her face, her worried tone spoke volumes. He came up behind her and massaged her shoulders again. "I was a bit of a bastard right then, trying to kiss you when members of your clan are dying. Tell me what to do to help you, Kaya-love, because I can't stand the thought of you being sad."

She turned her head toward him, her eyes vulnerable. If he had to guess, this was a side of Kaya she didn't show to many people.

As he stared into her eyes, she said, "Fuck it. After that, I need to hug you."

She stood up and turned to wrap her arms around him. He pulled her close and simply held her, reveling in her wild scent and heat invading his senses.

He stroked her hair for a few seconds before she let out a long sigh and said against his chest, "What if they all die? I've been looking through Markgen's emails for hours, and I haven't found a single thing to help us. On top of that, my researchers still don't have a stable, reliable cure or vaccine." She looked up at him, her eyes full of worry. "I can't lose my clan, Sy. They're much more than just a responsibility; they're my family."

He moved a hand to stroke her back, hoping to calm both the woman and the wolf. "But your clan has you, and I doubt you'll give them up without a fight." He gave her a squeeze and released her. "Now, as for the finding what you need part, I can help with that. I grabbed an extra laptop when I was at DS Engineering today, so let's divvy up the emails. Two people going through them will help speed up the process."

Kaya smiled and his cougar purred in approval. "Help me find what I need to save my clan, and I will make it very worth your while, Sylas Murray."

He moved toward her, turned her around, and gave her ass a light slap. "Then what are we waiting for? Let's get started. The sooner we fix this mess, the sooner I can have your sexy, naked self in my bed."

Kaya laughed and they got to work.

~~~

Two hours later, Kaya blinked at what she'd just read on the screen in front of her and decided to read it one more time to double-check the information. But no, she had read it right the first time. "Son of a bitch."

Sy looked up from his laptop. "Did you find something?"

Kaya frowned at the computer screen and then looked up at Sy. "I think I know who has been helping the mysterious Markgen people sneak onto DarkStalker's land and release the infected wolves. It's Kevin Howard."

"I'm guessing he's one of yours and there's more to the story."

Kaya leaned back in her chair and twisted her long hair up off her neck. "He was the main contender for the clan leader position when it opened up three years ago. The betting odds put me as second most likely to get it, but he couldn't win the final clan-wide vote; I did. Despite his bruised ego, I never would've guessed he'd go from wanting to dedicate his entire life to the clan to wanting to destroy it."

"What did you find, exactly, that makes you think he wants to destroy it?"

Kaya released her hair and looked at the laptop in front of her. "Well, he's been corresponding with someone inside Markgen who goes by the name 'John Smith' and over the last few weeks, their emails have gone from one every few weeks to several a day."

"There must be more to it than that."

She glanced up and gave him a look. "I'm not done yet." Sy put his hands up in apology and Kaya looked back to her screen. "While the email is in slight code, the time and dates match up to the events of the wolf-shifter attack and the discovery of the infected pup."

"What do the emails say exactly that convince you it's this Kevin Howard guy?"

Kaya leaned forward and read from her computer. "Things like, 'The three packages were delivered to DS and accepted,' which I think is talking about the three wolf-shifters that attacked your brother on DarkStalker's land. Or, 'The smaller package and message were received by DS,' and that fits with when Kian discovered the infected wolf pup with the flash drive."

She looked up at Sy and continued, "Kevin should've been in Seattle over the course of the last two weeks, yet if 'DS' stands for DarkStalker, he's been on and off your clan's land instead of doing his duties here. Although, how he managed to do it without getting caught speaks volumes about his ability to hide in plain sight." She motioned with her hand. "And then there's Kevin's most recent email, from late last night, where he wanted to confirm that John Smith would fulfill his end of the bargain at the meeting with GreyFire Industries."

Sy sat very still. No doubt he'd started to put it together too. "And?"

"John Smith said yes, and the proof of the delivery should appear in 24-48 hours after the meeting is finished." Kaya took in a deep breath and exhaled. "I'm pretty sure the 'delivery' is the virus. That means they've infected me, Sylas, and unless we find a way to stop it, I'm going to die."

Sy reached across the table, took her hand, and squeezed it. "Then we'd better hurry the fuck up and find this Kevin Howard to make sure that doesn't happen. Do you know where he is?"

Kaya made herself focus on finding Kevin instead of worrying about how, if she was right, she would devolve into a mindless, purple-eyed wolf over the next week. "He's one of GreyFire's human company go-betweens, which is why I dismissed his emails at first and why I believed him when he said he had another meeting scheduled and couldn't go to the Markgen one with me. Unless he has run away, he should still be at the apartment GreyFire rents for clan members visiting companies here."

Sy squeezed her hand again. "Okay, then we should check the place out. But before that, tell me anything I should know about this guy."

Kaya took strength from Sy's touch, the warmth of his hand around hers allowing her to focus better on what needed to be done than what might happen. "Apart from his stellar ability to get in and out of places without being detected, there's not much else special about him. After I won the clan leadership three years ago, he went to Seattle for a few weeks to lick his wounds, but he came back and pledged his loyalty to me. After that, his behavior was perfect to the point I had him coordinating the sentries for a few years before establishing him as one of our human company go-betweens."

His behavior was exactly why it'd taken Kaya so long to piece the clues together. Kevin had been nothing but supportive since she had taken over the clan. He'd even once tried to ask her out on a date.

Now she was starting to wonder if he'd only done that to try to get close to her so he could get rid of her easier.

If—no, when—she solved all of this and was healthy again, Kaya was going to do a more thorough job of investigating her clan and try to delegate more. Her first task would be finding someone to root out all the rumors running around GreyFire. Who knew, maybe there had been word of Kevin's discontent months before this.

For now, she needed to think of the immediate future.

What she was about to say was risky, but it needed to be done. Laying her free hand on top of Sy's, she said, "Before we start planning on how to track Kevin, I want you to know that I'm not revoking the power share. If I succumb to the virus, you're going to be in charge, Sy, if you want it."

~~~

Sy stared into Kaya's deep brown eyes and couldn't miss the small amount of fear he saw there. Oh, to most people, she would look calm and collected, but not to him.

No, with him she was becoming less afraid to be vulnerable and express her true feelings.

What she was asking was huge, but there was really only one way to answer. He stood up, yanked Kaya off her chair, and wrapped his arms around her. As she melted against him, he said, "I'll help, Kaya-love, but I'm hoping it doesn't come to me taking over."

She leaned back so she could look up at him. "Why? So you don't have to swear off DarkStalker as your clan?"

He shook his head. "I love DarkStalker, but I very much want you to live more. The autumn celebration is coming up and I want to show you off to the world as mine."

Her eyes softened. "Oh."

That expression went straight to his heart, and Sy decided she'd better fucking live or he would raise some hell to get his revenge.

He took a deep breath to calm the fuck down. Then he brushed her cheek and placed a gentle kiss on her lips. Kaya's touch, as always, was a surefire way to ease his anger.

Threading his fingers through her hair, he said, "Now, about this Kevin Howard guy, I think I have a plan."

He waited to see if Kaya would dismiss him, but instead she said, "Let me hear it."

Kaya listened as he explained it. She eyed him for a second before she nodded. "Okay. I don't really like it, but I see your point."

He gave her a squeeze with his arms. "Don't worry; you'll get your chance to rip him a new one. We just need to catch him first." He gave her another kiss and released her. "Gather what you need. We'll leave in ten minutes."

As Kaya went into her room to gather supplies, Sy placed a call to a few DarkStalker comrades in the area that he could trust with his life. Everything needed to go off without a hitch, and while he couldn't have Aidan or Dani, he'd make do with the best available to him.

For now, his main aim was to capture and question Kevin Howard before Kaya started showing symptoms. The last thing either one of them wanted was for GreyFire to catch word of Kaya's sickness. Erika might be holding down the fort, but chaos could break loose any moment, which Kevin Howard could then pounce upon.

Chapter Thirteen

An hour and a half later, Sy and Kaya were sitting inside a borrowed car across the street from where Kevin Howard should be staying. Sy glanced to the clock on the car's dashboard and then over to Kaya. "It's seven forty-five p.m. He should've checked in by now."

Kaya looked at him. "For nearly a year, Kevin has routinely called me after every meeting he's had with a human company. Usually it's around seven thirty p.m., but not always. Give him some time."

Sy didn't like waiting, and it didn't help that his cougar was pacing around inside his head. Cougars were usually patient when it came to their prey, but it was different with Kaya involved. The cat part of him was starting to think of Kaya and her wolf as his, and he knew something was wrong and just wanted to make it right.

If only it were that simple. At least his people were in place and ready to go at his signal.

Kaya's cell phone rang. She glanced down at the screen and said, "It's Kevin." She clicked the receive button and said, "Hello?"

In the confines of the car, it was easy enough for Sy to hear Howard on the line as he replied, "Hey, Kaya. I'm just checking in. Sorry I'm late, but after the meeting, some of the humans wanted to go out for something to eat."

How could this man be so calm and normal? Sy was starting to understand how the bastard had fooled Kaya.

As if sensing his irritation, Kaya put up a hand and Sy forced himself to listen to her reply. "No problem. I always work late anyway. So, did everything go to plan?"

"Yes. I think I found a few more investors for our next research trial. I'll email the documents to you by tomorrow morning."

"That'll work. However, I'd like to go over some of the information from the last few weeks with you in person, if possible. I won't leave Seattle until tomorrow afternoon. Can we meet at GreyFire's apartment tomorrow around lunch?"

Howard didn't miss a beat. "Sure, that shouldn't be a problem."

Sy clenched his fists. The bastard. No doubt he was counting on Kaya's symptoms starting to show by then.

Kaya laid a hand on his leg. As she stroked his thigh, it helped to ease some of his anger. "Okay, sounds good. I'll see you tomorrow, Kevin. Good night."

"Night."

Kaya clicked off the phone and Sy asked, "Do you think he'll run?"

She shook her head. "I doubt it. He's probably counting on me to cancel tomorrow because of not feeling well. Even if I'm still able to function by around lunch tomorrow, he'll show. If he, indeed, wants to step in and take over GreyFire's leadership, he needs to be extra careful not to set off any red flags. He'll carry on as he's done for the last how many months he's been planning this."

"The bastard can act, I'll give him that. Do you have any idea when he'll show?"

She squeezed his thigh. "He sounded like he was on a headset, which means he's probably in the car and should be here before too much longer. Are your people ready?"

He laid a hand on top of hers and stroked her thumb with his own. "Yes. I have two people across the street in human form, and two in cat form hiding in the trees at the back of the apartment tower."

"Good." Kaya tossed her phone on the dashboard and then leaned against his shoulder. He moved his arm so he could wrap it around her. She sighed. "I'm starting to feel a little tired, Sy, and that's not normal as I'm usually a night owl."

He squeezed her shoulders and forced himself to remain calm for Kaya's sake. "Just hold on for a little while longer, little wolfie."

Kaya frowned up at him. "Wolfie? Please tell me that's not a new nickname. Because if I hear it again once I'm healthy, I will kick your ass."

Despite the possible outcome of Kaya dying, Sy couldn't help but laugh. He decided to lighten the mood a little. "I think we need a real rematch; you and me in the woods, no-holds-barred. If I win, I get to call you wolfie whenever I like."

"And if I win?"

"Oh, you think you'll win?"

Kaya punched him in the stomach and he faked a great injury.

She frowned. "Oh, buck up. With your slab of solid muscle that masquerades as a stomach, you didn't feel a thing. Unless you're starting to go soft, Murray."

He grinned. "There's definitely nothing soft about me right now."

Kaya blinked and he scented her arousal. He decided to not go further down that avenue as he didn't need to be distracted by thoughts of Kaya naked and straddling his lap inside the car.

To forget that mental picture, he said, "Okay, in the off-chance you do best me, what do you want?"

Kaya sat up a little and assessed him for a second before she said, "I want you to wear an 'I Heart Wolves' t-shirt to the upcoming celebration Kian and I are planning for our two clans."

He grinned. "You really are evil, aren't you?"

She brushed a hand against her chest and looked down at her nails. "Of course."

"Well, if you are intent on being evil, then so shall I." He moved his hand from her shoulder down to her side. "Until that rematch, I don't have to play fair."

Before she could move, he tickled her side and Kaya's laughter made both his human and cougar halves purr in contentment. He was finally realizing what he and Kaya had had before was nothing compared to now. They could be planning take-downs one minute, and he could be tickling her the next. Their teenage selves had been more interested in finding some trouble or sneaking into the forest to make-out. Whereas now, he loved how they could handle life and its responsibilities together as a team.

Did Kaya feel the same way as him? That they could tackle anything as long as they worked together? Once the threat of both Kevin Howard and Kaya getting sick was taken care of, he'd ask her.

For now, he was content to tickle his wolf-shifter. The laughing and teasing was something he had missed over the years.

Reclaiming the Wolf

After the army, he'd been tougher and more secretive than before, careful to hide his deepest wish to find a female he could love and who could also be his best friend. Someone with whom he never had to hold back and who would just let him be himself; not just with his easygoing side, but his serious, intelligent side too.

Kaya had been that person before, but even more so now. Her trust in him to capture Kevin Howard was proof both sides of her, both the wolf and the woman, trusted the older, more mature version of him.

If he was honest with himself, he could admit he was very much falling in love with her again, and the thought of her possibly dying if he failed was unacceptable.

He stopped tickling her and moved his free hand to her cheek. He turned her head to face him. She had a slightly irritated look on her face, but it disappeared as her eyes met his. She whispered, "Sy, what is it?"

~~~

Kaya had fully planned on scolding Sylas Murray for taking advantage, yet again, of one of her weaknesses. But as she met his eyes, she drew in a breath at the mixture of intensity and tenderness. The last time she'd seen that look, it had been right before Sy had told her he loved her.

But before he could say whatever was on his mind, Kaya noticed the dark-colored sedan Kevin had borrowed from GreyFire's inventory last week. She reluctantly pushed away from Sy's warm body and said, "That's him." She watched as the car pulled into the underground car garage under the apartment building and then looked back to Sy. "Get him for me, Sylas."

He nodded, leaned over to give Kaya a quick, possessive kiss, and then grabbed his small bag of supplies. Before he opened the door, he said, "I know you're starting to feel tired, but if I need back-up, can I still call on you?"

"Of course. Have someone let out a cougar howl and I'll come running."

He looked as if he wanted to say something else, but then he was gone.

It was up to Sylas Murray to give her clan the best chance of surviving this ordeal. A week ago, she might've resented it. But now, she was glad for the help. Especially since the pounding in her head was making it hard to concentrate on anything.

Judging by what the GreyFire researchers had found out about the virus, she would be out with a high fever before morning. She had long accepted that she would die one day, but she hoped Kevin Howard had information about a cure. Otherwise, Kaya would die just as she'd found someone she could see as her mate.

And yes, both the woman and the wolf wanted Sylas Murray as her mate.

It'd taken ten years and two stubborn heads, but time had, indeed, made them fit better together. As much as Kaya trusted Erika to watch over her clan, she could see herself trusting Sy more. With him, she didn't have to hide a weakness like with her other clan members; if she fell ill, Sy would step in and not think less of her for it. If she needed a hug and a shoulder to cry on, she knew he would hold her close and murmur in her ear before finding a way to make her smile.

The bastard would probably use her ticklish weakness against her until the day he died.

She smiled at the thought of them being seventy years old and Sy still tickling her, maybe with a few grown pups watching on, embarrassed by their parents' behavior. It was a future she'd started to think she'd never have. Provided she could beat this virus, it might just be possible. Especially since she felt pretty sure Sy felt the same way. His look before leaving had spoken volumes about his feelings.

If she were honest with herself, Kaya was more than half in love with him again. Not just the memory, but rather the man he'd become.

For now, however, she needed to focus and try to keep her pounding headache in check for as long as she could in case Sy needed her help.

Glancing across the street, she watched as Sy and two of his team members disappeared into the apartment building.

She kept her ears open for any cougar howls. She might be incapacitated soon, but for now, she was still in good enough shape to help her cougar-shifter if things went bad.

CHAPTER FOURTEEN

The keycard Kaya had provided worked without any issues, and Sy and his two clan members slipped inside the apartment building. Like most apartment towers in Seattle, you needed an electronic keycard to first get into the building, and then take the elevator to the correct floor.

As the elevator doors closed, he was grateful it was empty because he, Ginnie, and Matt together would scare just about any human, especially with Sy's current mood.

Kaya could die, and the man upstairs was the reason.

His cat wanted to rip out the wolf-shifter's throat, but the man half of Sy knew they needed Howard alive. At least, for now. Kevin Howard would face the Shifter Department of Justice soon enough.

The elevator dinged and the doors opened to the fifth floor. He motioned for Ginnie to guard the elevator and for Matt to go with him. Sy took out the sedative injector from his bag of goodies, and then he went down the left corridor to find apartment number 5D.

He found it, motioned for Matt to stay out of sight of the peephole, and then knocked. He heard someone approach the door and say, "Who is it?"

Sy resisted the urge to smooth his borrowed power company uniform. "I'm with Seattle Energy. There's been a reported gas leak in this building, and I need to do a quick gas reading and ask you a few questions."

He expected Howard to open the door, but it remained shut. "I smell some kind of feline-shifter. Why are you here?"

Sy kept his cool. "Seattle Energy has started a new program, employing shifter-liaisons part-time to help ease both sides. Too many of Seattle Energy's human employees are afraid to even talk to one of us."

Howard paused, and then said, "True. I'm surprised Seattle Energy waited this long to do something about it. The cable company needs to follow suit." He heard the lock start to turn. "Have your credentials out when I open the door."

Oh, Sy had his "credentials" ready; his injector was in his hand under the clipboard.

The lock clicked open, but the door didn't move. That didn't surprise Sy. Considering the years Kevin had patiently waited to find a way to take over the clan, he'd expected the man to have some caution and intelligence.

He signaled Matt to loosen his clothes and be ready to shift. Then Sy slowly turned the doorknob and opened the door an inch. He could smell the male wolf-shifter, but he couldn't hear anything. Either Howard was right behind door, or hiding around a corner.

Kaya had drawn the apartment layout for him earlier, so he knew what to expect. Sy tightened his grip on the sedative injector, and kicked opened the door.

The next ten seconds were like a blur. Howard in wolf form jumped from around the corner and tried to take out Sy's neck. But the split second before he could make contact, Sy used his metal clipboard box to whack the shifter on the side of his head. Since Sy needed to stay in human form to use the injector, he whistled and Matt jumped into the room in his cougar form just in time to tackle the wolf to the ground.

As the pair wrestled on the floor, Sy gave another whistle. Once he heard Ginnie running down the hallway, he watched Matt and Howard on the floor, waiting for his opening. While a cougar didn't stand a chance against a pack of wolves, a lone wolf was no match for a healthy, adult cougar.

He heard Ginnie stop behind him and shut the door to keep the shifter fight away from prying eyes. They both watched Matt wrestling on the floor. Howard's moves were sluggish; the wolf was getting tired.

Then Matt managed to pin the wolf on the floor and keep him in place by fastening his jaw around the wolf-shifter's neck. Sy rushed forward at the same time as Ginnie. He grabbed the wolf-shifter's leg, pressed the injector against his skin, and filled the wolf with a sedative.

After about thirty seconds, Howard went limp. Sy said to Ginnie, "Open the balcony. The other two should be waiting in the trees outside."

She moved to the back door and he gave Matt's side a pat. "Good job, Matt. Once the other two come in, they can watch over the wolf-shifter while you get dressed. I need you to help me search the place for Howard's laptop and any other promising clues."

While he kept the wolf-shifter pinned under his body, Matt released his grip on Howard's jaw and gave a low chirp just as two adult cougars trotted across the floor. Sy stood up and looked at the two DarkStalker cougars that had just entered the apartment. "Okay, while it's unlikely he'll wake up, I want you two to watch over the wolf while Ginnie, Matt, and I search the place. Make a sound if he moves."

The two cougars nodded and Sy turned to Ginnie. "I want you to search the kitchen." Matt finished shifting back to his human form. He was naked, but shifters didn't pay much attention to that. "Matt, take the bedroom. I'll search the living room."

His clan members nodded and Sy went to work.

~~~

Kaya sat in the car, rubbing her temples, and resisted looking at the clock on the stereo console for the hundredth time. Even in her slightly unwell state, her wolf was pacing and itching to go join the fight to capture Kevin Howard so they could try to find a way to save GreyFire. An alpha's duty was to protect the pack.

But the human-half of Kaya knew better. Taking a sick wolf into battle would end up getting multiple people killed.

She only hoped Sy was successful. His reasoning about how Kaya showing up unannounced at Kevin's door could make the wolf-shifter suspicious, and possibly reach out to his contact at Markgen before talking with her, made sense.

This would be the first real test of how her wolf handled letting the cougar-shifter briefly take charge, and also to see how Sy handled stepping in when needed and handing the reins back to her afterward. If he couldn't transfer the power and decisions back, she would die a little inside because she'd have no choice but to push him away.

Her wolf snarled; she didn't like the idea of letting the male cougar-shifter go.

Kaya smiled at that. Her wolf had refused more than a few wolf-shifters from her clan, but seemed intent on keeping the feline nearby. Oh, how her uncle would've had a heart attack at that revelation.

Movement at the apartment tower's entrance caught her eye. A tall woman with red hair peeked out, looked around, and strode with the grace of a cat toward where Kaya was sitting in the car. The woman unlocked the doors with the electronic key lock, opened the driver's side door, and slid in. She closed the door and said, "I'm Ginnie from DarkStalker. Sy's waiting with Kevin Howard, and he sent me to drive over to collect them." She looked Kaya in the eye. "May I drive your car?"

Ginnie's brown eyes were steady, belying her role as a soldier or sentry for DarkStalker. Neither half of Kaya sensed a threat, and since her head was pounding even worse now, she nodded and said, "Go ahead."

The woman nodded, turned the key in the ignition, and pulled the car into the street.

Two minutes later, Ginnie stopped in front of the building entrance and exited the car. Rather than risk being caught on any of the security cameras, or worse, losing her balance when she stood up due to her pounding head, Kaya stayed inside.

The rear door opened and despite the mixture of feline and wolf scents that bombarded her nose, it was Sy's masculine scent she picked out first. She turned in her seat and he met her eyes, a triumphant look in his. "Hey, Kaya. Guess what the cat brought in?"

She groaned at his joke. "Putting aside your corny joke, are you going to tell me what happened?"

"Just a second."

Sy maneuvered the unconscious wolf into the car, his wonderful muscles bunching and flexing with the effort, just as someone else opened the trunk and she heard something tossed inside. With Kevin strapped in, Sy allowed a male in cougar form to jump into the backseat. No doubt, to act as a guard on the off chance Kevin woke up.

The rear door slammed closed, and a second later, Sy opened the driver's side door and slid in. Not caring about the cougar watching them in the backseat, he took hold of her neck and pulled her close for a gentle kiss. Then he said, "Now I can talk."

She gave him a playful pat and reluctantly, he moved away to start the car. As he pulled out onto the street, she said, "So?"

"Well, there wasn't any bottle with 'Antidote' written on it, but we did take his laptop, cell phone, briefcase, and a few files we found in his apartment." He glanced at Kaya. "I was thinking, once we switch cars, we could take it all back to GreyFire and assign a team to help look through everything. That would speed up the process. What do you think?"

The question was asking her permission. Her wolf wanted to lick his face in gratitude for all but handing power back into her hands.

Aware of their audience in the backseat, however, she cleared her throat and said, "That's exactly what I would've done. I can set things in motion on the drive up, if you don't mind driving?"

Sy's eyes were back on the road, but she saw the smile on his face. She could tell he was itching to tease her, but true to his word, he didn't embarrass her, even if it was his clan member and not hers in the back seat. "No. But how would you feel about letting Matt back there, along with Ginnie, the redhead from earlier, take Howard up in a separate car? I'd rather divide up and lessen the risk of an attack if for some reason someone decides to track Howard's cell phone or computer."

And he left unsaid the other big reason—to prevent anyone from seeing how sick she would become.

She wasn't used to someone looking out for her, and it felt...nice. She didn't doubt for a second that Sy would take care of her once her fever showed up.

Focus, Kaya. She wasn't about to worry if she'd ever wake up or not once that happened. She was awake now, and she had things to do. She said, "I can give your team the location of a remote sentry shelter at the edge of GreyFire's land. That way, if someone is tracking the bastard, they'll see Kevin's on GreyFire's land, but they won't find the heart of my den." She turned to look into Matt's blue cougar eyes. "Provided, first, that Matt doesn't mind working with the wolves. Shake your head if you don't mind doing so."

The cougar tilted his head in the feline way for a second to study her, but while his blue gaze was strong, she was stronger. Eventually, he blinked and then he shook his head.

Kaya smiled. "Good." She turned back toward Sy. "Let me call Kian and double-check that it's okay to borrow his clan members for a spell."

As she took out her phone and started dialing, Sy reached out and gave her thigh a squeeze. She looked over at him. His eyes were full of approval and something tender, and the sight made her heart skip a beat.

He is ours, her wolf said inside her head. And yes, Kaya agreed. Sylas Murray was theirs, and no matter how sick she became, she was going to fight her damnedest to get well again so she could tell him that. Then, to make up for too many years apart, she would ask him to fuck her until she couldn't stand, and she knew he would do it, too. With Sy, she'd never have to worry about someone only wanting her because of her position, let alone worry about a man treating her as a fragile thing about to break. Despite the fact they'd only reconnected less than a week ago, he knew her better than just about anyone else.

She was falling for him again.

Kian's voice came over the phone and she reluctantly broke her gaze to concentrate on what the other clan leader was saying. She needed to get everything going in both the GreyFire and DarkStalker clans while she still had the ability to do so.

Chapter Fifteen

For the hundredth time, Sy resisted the urge to pull over the car, move Kaya into his lap, and try to soothe her. She'd fallen asleep about an hour ago, and ever since, she had been moving and twitching in her seat, as if she were fighting off a nightmare.

He'd tried talking to her, switching on relaxing music, and even caressing her with his free hand, but none of that had worked. He was pretty confident he knew why.

The virus was starting to attack Kaya with full force.

His inner cat growled. He wanted something tangible to fight off to protect their wolf-shifter. The animal-half of him didn't understand this invisible enemy. Of course, his human-half did, and it scared the living shit out of him.

Kaya could die.

Sy gripped the steering wheel tighter, and tried to calm down his inner cougar. If the cat didn't get his irritation under control, Sy wouldn't be able to use his brain as effectively to take care of the wolves and, more importantly, Kaya.

He had made the final turn onto GreyFire's land a few minutes ago, which meant they'd be at the den in about twenty minutes. The sooner he could get Kaya to her people, the sooner they could see if they could make her comfortable. He only hoped they were making progress on the cure.

His phone rang. Sy saw it was his brother, so he clicked the receive button on his ear piece, grateful for the distraction. "Yeah, Kian? What's up?"

"I had one of our people, Rivera, keep an eye on GreyFire's place in Seattle and someone came to do more than pay a call—they broke into the apartment."

Good thing they'd searched and stripped the place first. "Tell me the rest."

"Rivera tailed the middle-aged man back to Markgen, but the man has yet to come back out again."

"Did Rivera get a picture of this guy?"

"Yeah. It's a bit grainy, but I've sent it to your phone. Can you get Kaya to look at it right now and see if she recognizes him?"

Sy glanced over at the wolf-shifter, who was currently whimpering softly in her seat. He decided his brother had a right to know what was going on. Especially since some of DarkStalker's people were involved with helping the wolves. "Are you alone right now, Kian?"

Something in Sy's voice must've given away that something wrong because Kian's voice became concerned. "Yes, it's just me in my office. What's up little brother?"

He decided he didn't have the spirit to argue with his twin brother about him being older by a few minutes. Instead, he took a deep breath and said, "I think Kaya caught the virus."

Kian's line went quiet for a second before he replied. "How did it happen? Wasn't she clean when she left GreyFire?"

"Yes, but somehow a Dr. John Smith at Markgen found a way to infect not just her, but her two researchers as well. We think it was either in the air or the drinks they had while waiting for him."

"How bad is she?"

Only because Sy was driving did he keep his eyes on the road instead of pulling Kaya into his lap to hold close. "Her fever started a little over an hour ago and she's now unconscious. I think she's having nightmares since she keeps whimpering and moving around." He glanced quickly at Kaya and then back to the road again. "She might die, Kian, and I'm not sure I can save her."

"That's the bitch of loving someone, brother—sometimes things are out of your hands and there's nothing you can do to save them."

Sy didn't even try to deny he loved Kaya. Instead, he decided he needed to tell his brother the whole truth. "There's something else you should know, Kian, before I get to GreyFire and try to contain the situation."

"Hm?"

"Kaya declared a power share with me."

Kian was quiet for a few seconds before he said, "You're full of surprises today, Sylas. You know that once you step on GreyFire's land and accept the power share that you forfeit your guardian position, as well as you clan membership, with DarkStalker. Are you sure that's what you want?"

If he accepted the power share on GreyFire's land, it was final. Per tradition, he'd be kicked out of DarkStalker, maybe for good.

Kaya cried out in the seat beside him. He reached out a hand to rub her leg, and this time she did quiet down a little. Even so, each small cry of pain felt like a knife stabbing into his heart.

As he rubbed his wolf-shifter's thigh, he knew he couldn't let her down. Kaya had trusted him enough to declare the power share, and he would see it through if it killed him.

Considering Kaya had an incurable virus, death was a real possibility if her clan ended up blaming Sy for her death.

Don't think about that. There was still time to try to save his wolf's life.

Gripping the steering wheel tight, he said, "Kaya entrusted me with her clan, and I'm not about to screw that up. No matter what it takes, I won't let her down this time."

"I think I'm about to shed a tear. My little brother has finally become a man."

He growled. "Will you ever stop lording those five minutes over me, asshole?"

"Never, my twin." Sy heard a knock on the other end of the line and Kian's voice was muted, as if he'd put the phone down. A second later Kian's voice came back on the line. "Find someone in GreyFire who can identify the picture I sent you as soon as possible and then have someone call me back if you can't do it."

"Sure thing. Thanks, Kian."

"No problem, brother. Don't hesitate to call me if you need help. Even though you'll reek of wolf from now on, I'll still find a way to love you."

Sy almost smiled. Before he could say anything, his sister-in-law's voice came on the line. "Kian has something he needs to attend to, and I wanted to talk to you before you get so busy that you can't spare two seconds for me."

He resisted a sigh and steeled himself for his sister-in-law's meddling. "What did you want to tell me, Trin?"

"Just take care of Kaya. I like her."

He growled without thinking. "Of course I'm going to take care of her. I'm not sure why you would think I wouldn't. Is that what you wanted to tell me?"

"Well, I was going to tell you something useful about blood donors for transfusions. Did you want to hear it or are you just going to growl at me again?"

"Make it quick, Trin. I'm nearly at GreyFire's secret back entrance."

"Okay, Mr. Cheerful. I've made a list of all the cougar-shifters who've had contact with the infected but who don't have any symptoms and are healthy. If you need any more blood transfusions from them, just ask. You may be GreyFire now, but you'll always be my brother-in-law. I have faith in you to set this right."

"How did you know I was GreyFire now? Kian said he was alone."

"Don't worry; your brother didn't lie to you about being alone. It was obvious to me how you and Kaya fit together. It was only a matter of time until we lost you."

"Trin..."

"Neither of us has time for sentimental bullshit. Take care of your female, Sy, and let Kian and I know if you need our help."

"Thanks, Trin. Talk to you soon, I promise."

"Bye, Sylas."

The phone clicked off and he couldn't believe how lucky he was to have Kian as his brother and Trinity as his sister-in-law. They barely blinked an eye at his changing clans and loving a wolf-shifter.

Things were a lot different than they'd been ten years ago, and not just because of him and Kaya being ten years older. No, for the first time, he actually believed the different shifter clans could be close allies.

He approached the last few turns to his destination and pushed those thoughts away. He didn't want to miss a turn and get lost.

He had never driven to GreyFire's hidden entrance and he was relying entirely on the directions he'd received earlier from Kaya. He needed to concentrate. Every second he spent getting lost would be a second less of time for Kaya to get help from one of her clan healers or her clan researchers.

But as soon as one of GreyFire's vehicles came into view, he knew he'd arrived at the right place.

He pulled next to the other vehicle and just as he exited the car, Erika Washington strode out of the door from the den. "Sylas. Where's Kaya?"

He moved toward the passenger's side of the car. "I overheard her talking to you on our way here, so you know what's going on." He didn't say it, but Erika nodded in understanding about Kaya being sick. He leaned close to Erika and said, "Is there a way to get inside without everyone seeing?"

Erika stilled a second at his proximity, no doubt her wolf trying to figure out if he was a threat or not. Kaya's second didn't have any symptoms—yet. Their best guess as to why was due to the fact that Erika's grandfather had been human, which was rare among the shifters of the Cascade Mountains. But the slightly different DNA could be protecting her.

She nodded. "Get back into the car and give me a few minutes. I'll bring two of our most trusted doctors out as well."

Sy didn't like waiting, but he knew they needed to avoid a panic. A sick, unconscious, and restless Kaya would start a surge of worry and maybe even hysteria. During his tours in Iraq, he'd seen firsthand the effects a death or sickness of a leader could have on a population or family. He wasn't about to start that here.

He nodded and headed back to the driver's side. Once he was in his seat, he turned toward Kaya and cupped her cheeks. Her skin was burning to the touch, but he kept his hold and started to strum his thumb back and forth against her skin. This might be the only chance they had alone for quite a while, so he said, "Fight for me, Kaya-love. There's so much we could do together. And besides, I want you awake when I tell you that I love you." He leaned down and placed a gentle kiss on her warm lips. "Don't die on me, Kaya Geraldine Alexie. I'm not sure I can survive being without you again."

~~~

Kaya stood in the middle of GreyFire's main hall. The only light came from the main hall's entrance on the far side of the room, and the smell of death permeated the air. At first, she could barely make out more than vague shapes in the dark, but then the lights flickered on and Kaya stopped breathing.

Erika lay on her back with her eyes closed and her throat slashed open. Turning the other way, she saw Jonathan was chained up in wolf-form, his eyes glowing an eerie purple. A few feet away from him, a couple held their dead child in their arms, crying and wailing the way only a parent could when they had lost their baby.

Despite the tightness in her chest, she forced herself to keep looking around the room. As she slowly turned and surveyed the surroundings, the situation was the same everywhere. Clan members were dying, dead, grieving, or chained up with glowing purple eyes.

She couldn't hold back her emotions anymore, and shock, denial, anger, sadness, and a bevy of other feelings coursed through her. Her clan was dying and she didn't know how to save them.

She'd failed them.

Reclaiming the Wolf

She tried calling Sy's name, but she didn't see him anywhere. Had he abandoned her? Or was he also dead? She didn't like either option, but she hoped it wasn't the former because it would only highlight how she'd come to trust him too soon. Also, it meant he'd deserted her when she needed him most.

Again.

She took a deep breath and tried to focus on what she could do rather than what she couldn't change.

First things first, she needed to reach her office and see if she could call Kian to ask for his help. Provided, of course, he hadn't also abandoned her. Without the cougars, her clan's chances of rebuilding or survival were nearly zero.

Kaya tried to move toward the corridor to go to her office, but after walking just a few feet, flames started sprouting up all around her. She tried moving her legs to get away, but they wouldn't budge. She was stuck in place.

The flames licked her skin, burning her with each caress, and she battled a scream. Then the flames engulfed her completely and all she could feel was pain, so much pain. She had no words to describe it.

Her last thought as the flames consumed her was how she'd failed her clan. GreyFire was no more.

Kaya's eyes opened on the tail end of a scream. The room was bright, but there weren't any flames. And yet her skin was still burning.

Where the hell was she?

Sy's face came into her vision and she felt some relief. He was here. He hadn't abandoned her.

He touched her forehead and worry flickered in his eyes. "Kaya?"

159

She tried to sit up, but her body felt heavy. Maybe if she could cool down, she could make her body work. She would ask for Sy's help. "Hot. Sy, I'm so hot. I want to be cool."

He caressed her cheek, his voice a little unstable. "I know, baby. Wait here. I'll get you a cool cloth."

He moved, leaving her alone. She tried to kick off the covers, but she could barely move her toes, let alone her legs. Terror filled her at the thought she was dying, but then she pushed it back. Even with a fever and her inability to move much, Kaya's stubbornness would never disappear.

Sy came back, laid something cool and wet on her forehead, and she let out a sigh.

Somehow, despite the fuzziness and the burning, her mind started to function a little. She remembered Sy driving her to her clan's land, but she must've fallen unconscious at some point because the room she lay in was familiar. This was one of the sick rooms inside GreyFire's den.

She looked into Sy's eyes and she found strength in his tender, warm gaze. Sylas Murray had stayed by her side and taken care of her. She couldn't give in to her sickness. She needed to be strong, for him and their future.

She managed to mumble, "How long have I been out?"

Sy ran another cool cloth over her cheek and neck. The motion helped to soothe her wolf, who was weak and angry at not being able to move, let alone run through the clan's den to assess the situation.

His voice was rough when he finally spoke. "About three hours. One inside the car, and two here."

She licked her dry lips and Sy noticed. He put down the cloth and picked up a small cup of water. He raised her head and she took a few sips before closing her eyes. If taking a drink of water was a chore, Kaya knew it wouldn't be long before she was unconscious again. She needed to make sure things were in place.

She opened her eyes and said, "Sy. Give me a report."

The corner of his mouth ticked up. "Even with a raging fever and lethargy, you're still bossy." Before she could muster the strength for a reply, he leaned down and gave her a gentle kiss. Kaya sighed, the warm touch of his lips making her feel a little better.

Sy took one of her hands in his and started talking again. "After two hours of questioning and some light 'persuasion', Kevin Howard is still resisting. The only thing Matt and Ginnie found out so far is how the threat of locking him up with infected wolf-shifters didn't make him bat an eye. He quite proudly said he was immune. So a team of your researchers went to draw blood and various samples for their work."

At least they knew there was a vaccine or cure of some sort. Since speaking took a lot of energy, she kept her response short. "Progress on research?"

He squeezed her hand. "One of the wolves from the first round of cougar-shifter blood transfusions appears to be getting better. The other three in the group are still inconclusive. As for a vaccine or cure, no nothing yet."

Then Kaya knew what she needed to do. "If they don't find anything within the next day, I want the transfusion."

Sy's eyes turned fierce. "You should wait at least three days. There's a high chance the transfusion will kill you. I'd rather give your medical team more time to find a safer approach."

"Three might be too late. Two."

He shook his head. "Fine. Two. Why I love your stubbornness, I'll never understand. It makes my life difficult."

She smiled, and without thinking, she said, "You know you love me."

He stilled a second and Kaya wondered if she'd just made a mistake. After all, who wanted to be saddled with a dying girlfriend?

Then he moved his free hand to her cheek and hope started to gather in her chest. His voice was fierce yet tender when he said, "Damn straight I love you. So get your sexy ass well so I can show you how much."

Chapter Sixteen

Sy hadn't planned to tell Kaya that he loved her yet, but he hadn't been able to stop himself.

The few seconds between getting the words out and waiting for Kaya's response were some of the longest seconds of his life. Then Kaya let out a sigh and said, "Sy. Kiss me."

He hated how weak she sounded. Again, his inner cougar wanted to do something, anything, to save her and he had to stroke his cat to calm him down. Then Sy leaned down and stopped a hairbreadth from her lips. "Tell me, Kaya-love. I want to hear it."

He stared into her eyes, but she never looked away. No, his wolf-shifter would never shy away from him, which was another reason he loved her.

The heat of her breath danced along his lips as she whispered, "I love you, Sylas."

He growled and kissed her. He should be gentle, but the instant his lips touched hers, something snapped inside of him.

Not that Kaya minded as she opened her mouth and let his tongue stroke hers. Distracted by the silky heat of her mouth, it took him a second to realize her mouth was too hot, way too hot.

Because she had a fever.

No. You need to take care of her. He reluctantly retreated, kissed her lips, and then laid his forehead against hers. "What can I do to help you, love?"

In a second, he felt a hand in his hair. Sy rubbed a hand up and down Kaya's arm and she said, "Visit Kevin Howard and see what you can find out."

His hand stilled on her arm and he gave her a light squeeze. "I don't want to leave you."

"You must, for our clan."

For our clan. Her words sent a thrill through his body. Kaya already believed he was part of GreyFire now.

He lifted his head so he could look into her beautiful brown eyes. "Only if you promise me you'll try your damnedest to stay alive. I don't want to come back and find you gone."

She gave a weak smile. "Are you really going to question my stubbornness?"

He chuckled. "Of course not." He kissed her nose. "And I promise if there's no progress on a cure in two days, I'll see you get the transfusion. Provided our blood types are compatible, I'll give you my own. Then you'll always have my blood running through your veins."

Kaya blinked her eyes and then cleared her throat. "Sylas Murray, you can be romantic when you try."

He grinned. "You haven't seen anything yet."

She laughed and a rush of happiness shot through his body. How had he ever left this female in the first place? He'd been a fucking idiot, that's for sure.

This time he wasn't letting her go. He very much looked forward to her being whole and healthy again so he could show her how much she meant to him with his lips, his hands, and his cock. While he'd like a week, he'd have to make do with less until GreyFire was back on its feet again.

Sy gave her one last quick kiss and then forced himself to stand up. Brushing a few strands of hair off Kaya's forehead, he said, "I love you, Kaya Alexie, and you'd better fucking be alive when I come back."

She never broke eye contact. "And you'd better be ready for a mate when you get back, because I'm not letting you go."

Sy's heart skipped a beat. "A mate?"

A bit of her confidence faltered. "Unless you don't want me."

So Kaya was initiating the mate claim. His inner cat rumbled in approval. "Of course I want you." He cupped her cheek. "And this time, I'm here for the long haul."

The happiness in her eyes reached all the ways to his heart. "Good. Now kiss me and get the fuck out of here."

He laughed. Then he leaned over, gave her a slow, lingering kiss, and stood up. "I'll be back, Kaya-love. But if you need something to think about while you're stuck in bed, then try to imagine the roughest, hardest sex of your life because that's what I plan to do to you once you're well."

She blinked. "Okay."

He grinned, gave her hand a squeeze, and with great effort, forced himself to turn and walk out the door. *Don't worry. Her stubborn ass will stay alive for you, Murray.* He sure as hell hoped so.

Once in the hall, he switched his mind into work mode and double-checked that it was just Erika and the two doctors before he said, "I'm going to pay Kevin Howard a visit. Can you arrange for someone to meet me outside the hidden entrance to take me to his location?"

Erika nodded. "Sure. But technically, with Kaya ill, you're in charge. We really should make an announcement."

Sy shook his head. "Not yet. Kaya is still able to make decisions if need be and the transfer of power might cause more problems than the clan can handle right now."

Erika studied him for a second and then said, "I may have been wrong about you."

"So we can quit all this questioning me bullshit from now on?"

"I'll try, but if it's something I think could harm Kaya, I may call you out on it."

His cougar growled at the idea of hurting Kaya. "Since hurting her is the last thing I ever want to do, I don't think it's necessary. But if I slip, then by all means, call me out on it."

Erika put out a hand and Sy took it. After shaking, he released her hand and tapped his cell phone in his pocket. "Keep me in contact. If anything, and I mean anything, goes wrong with Kaya, call me so I can come straight back."

The female wolf-shifter nodded. "And let me know if you get anything new out of the traitor."

Sy's cougar approved of the venom in Erika's voice. "Oh, I'll get him to talk. Any man who hurts the woman I love will damn well learn his lesson."

With that, he turned and headed toward the secret entrance.

~~~

An hour later, after driving to the edge of GreyFire's land, Sy entered the sentry shelter serving as a holding pen. The two DarkStalker cougars, Ginnie and Matt, nodded to him in greeting, and then Sy looked into the blue eyes of the wolf-shifter who had turned traitor.

The wolf had a bruise on one of his cheeks, and despite Sy's intentions to remain calm, his cougar chirped in approval. The bastard deserved so much more.

He was careful to keep his expression neutral. For now, he needed to observe and assess Howard before he could decide how to interrogate him. His time in the army had taught him there were many techniques he could employ from the Army Field Manual without committing torture.

While he knew Matt had slugged Howard in self-defense earlier, it would be too easy for Sy to release his anger by beating the shit of the male who'd hurt Kaya.

Still, he was better than that. No matter how much he hated the wolf for his role in making Kaya sick, he wouldn't torture him.

He kept his voice level as he said to Howard, "You and I are about to have a conversation." He glanced at his—now former?—clan members and said, "Join the two wolves outside and wait for me."

Used to taking orders from him, they nodded. Once the door clicked closed behind them, Sy trained his green-eyed gaze on Howard and decided to start with attacking the wolf-shifter's ego and pride to see how he reacted. "I've never met a shifter with such self-hatred of being a shifter that he'd try to eradicate an entire clan just to gain some human's acceptance."

Howard growled. "I don't care about any human's acceptance."

He raised an eyebrow. "Then you seriously need to let your loss of the clan leader position to Kaya go. It's been three years, buddy."

Howard's eyes widened just a fraction, but Sy had been paying close enough attention to catch it. Howard's voice remained calm when he answered, "I think you've mistaken me for someone else."

Sy took the wooden chair from the nearby desk, turned it around, and sat in it backwards. "So if I brought in the two GreyFire wolves who accompanied me here, they would say you never wanted to be clan leader?"

Howard stared at him, and Sy stared back. Not saying anything was an effective strategy.

After about a minute, Howard finally said, "What do you want?"

"Well, for starters, where to find the cure. Threats about bringing in sick wolves doesn't seem to faze you, so somehow you're immune and I'd like to know how."

"Sure. And then you'd magically let me go." He gave a strangled laugh. "No, I want a guarantee for my safety and an assurance of escape before I even consider helping you."

Sy raised an eyebrow. "And where would you run to? My brother is all set to release your name, photograph, and a summary of your betrayal to every clan on the planet; no clan will take you in. If anything, they might kill you for betraying your kind. Add that to the human enforcers from the Shifter Department of Justice being on the lookout for you, and face it, Howard, you're fucked."

"Then why help you at all?"

Sy leaned forward. "Because there is a whole pack of wolves ready to mete out the old brand of shifter-style justice; I can at least guarantee you'll live long enough to be handed over to the human authorities."

Reclaiming the Wolf

"And why would you do that? You don't seem like the compassionate type."

"Because, wolf, I'd much rather have you rot in jail for the next five or six decades. Death is too easy an out."

Howard fell quiet for a minute to consider his words. Sy recognized the instant when the man realized his circumstances and what his chances were at escaping a brutal shifter-style death. Shifters may be civilized now, but it hadn't always been that way. Old-style justice meant slowly being torn to pieces.

Finally, Howard said, "I'm supposed to take a cougar's word because why?"

Sy relaxed his forearms on the chair's back and fought the urge to throw the wolf-shifter across the room. "Kaya declared a power share with me. I'm your new clan leader, asshole, so my word is the only one that matters right now."

To the wolf's credit, Howard didn't just take him at his word and he actually looked rather unconvinced. But Howard was teetering, and with a little more proof of Sy's position and words, the wolf-shifter might just accept his fate and cooperate.

He might be able to save Kaya.

Sy whipped out his cell phone and dialed Erika. When she picked up, he said, "Are you alone?"

"For now, yes. I'm in the hallway. Did you find out anything?"

He switched his cell to speakerphone even though Howard could probably hear the conversation anyway and said, "Erika, tell Howard here who is technically in charge of GreyFire now."

Erika paused a beat, but thankfully her mind was quick and she trusted him enough to answer, "You are. Kaya declared a power share with you."

"Thanks, that's all I need to know."

He clicked off the phone and looked Howard right in the eye. "Your fate is in my hands, Kevin Howard. So how about we try this again?"

Howard remained silent. Sy extend his claws on one hand and said, "Or, as clan leader, I might take up my right to challenge you to a fight in shifter form." He extended his claws on his other hand. "And a single wolf against a cougar doesn't stand a chance."

Howard said, "Killing me won't help you."

"I said nothing about killing. But you can A) cooperate and go to jail, B) I can humiliate your ass first, and then you can go to jail, or C) I just say fuck it and let the wolves have you. Which will it be?"

"And how is jail supposed to protect me from Markgen? You have no idea what you're meddling with, cougar."

Sy's patience was getting short. He stood up and stared down at the wolf, letting his cougar show in his eyes. "You do realize that unless we find a cure, Markgen can blackmail any canine-shifter pack in the world, right? Is your bruised ego really worth it? You can either be the traitor who eventually helped protect the world's canine-shifters, or you can be the traitor who threatened, and possibly killed, them all. That's quite a legacy to leave behind for you and any family you have."

Sy hoped his tactic paid off. Playing to the wolf-shifter's ego seemed to be the only thing that worked with him, at least, so far.

He never broke Howard's blue-eyed gaze. The instant Sy saw a flash of defeat he knew he had him.

Howard said, "I have a condition first."

Sy raised an eyebrow. "Are you really in a position to make demands?"

Narrowing his eyes, Howard spat out, "Even if you toss me to the wolves and they rip me to pieces, if I don't talk first, most everyone here will die without a cure. I'd say it's fair to give me something in return."

The wolf didn't deserve shit, but Sy could at least humor the male. If he lied, Sy would talk with the Shifter Department of Justice about a harsher punishment. "I can't promise anything, but what do you want?"

Howard sat up as straight as he could with his hands tied behind his back. "I want to be imprisoned with the DarkStalker cougars rather than a human-run shifter jail."

He could see why the man would ask for that. As soon as word got out about why Howard was in prison, he was as good as dead. Nothing the humans did to ensure his safety would be enough for any pissed off shifter hell-bent on revenge. Even if no one in his future jail had relations in the Cascade Mountains, canine-shifters tended to look out for one another.

A very small part of him liked that idea, but he pushed it aside. Sy meant what he had said earlier about death being too easy a sentence for the wolf-shifter who had put Kaya's life in danger.

Besides, agreeing might give Howard more of an incentive to tell the truth. "Provided both DarkStalker and the Shifter Department of Justice agree, then it may be possible."

Howard said, "I want you to call your brother now and find out."

The urge to punch the wolf-shifter in the face grew stronger. "Not until you give me something first, as a down payment of good faith."

The wolf-shifter shook his head. "No. I give you anything, and you'll just keep at me until I give it all up. Now, call your brother."

Sy studied the man for a second and decided he was done with the negotiating bullshit. He stood up and said, "I've been patient, but I no longer have time for your shit." He made his way to the door and placed his hand on the doorknob. "Previously, the wolves had their orders not to harm you, but I'm going to rescind that order and let them back in here. I'm sure they can think of ways to make you talk, especially since their wolves are probably itching to draw blood."

Sy turned the doorknob, opened the door, and shouted, "Any shifters out here want to take their turn with the traitor, with no rules or restrictions on how you extract information?"

All four shifters outside, two cougars and two wolves, shouted, "Yes," before they rushed inside the shelter.

As they surrounded Howard, Sy said, "Let me know when he talks."

The instant he stepped a foot outside the shelter, Howard screamed and then said, "Wait."

He resisted a smile and turned back toward the wolf-shifter, who now had a red claw mark across his cheek. "Yes?"

"If you took my briefcase from the apartment, there's a hidden pouch with a tiny vial of clear liquid. That was my back-up vial in case the one I received didn't work."

He raised an eyebrow and kept his feelings tightly in control. He didn't want to get his hopes up too early. "You just happen to have an extra vial of the cure laying around?"

"No. I wanted a back-up, not just for me, but for my sister as well."

Sy would investigate the sister claim later. For now, he asked, "And it's just two doses?"

Howard shook his head. "There should be enough for three. I wasn't taking any chances."

Except with everyone else's lives, but Sy didn't say that. "How long will it take for the cure to start working?"

"I was injected before I got sick. But from what I've been told, it should start working on a sick wolf in about four hours."

Sy nodded. "Okay, then I'm going to test it out. If what you say is true, I'll come back and we can talk to my brother."

Before Howard could protest, Sy was out the door. Closing it behind him, he headed back to his car. If Howard was telling the truth, then all he had to do was test the cure on a volunteer and hope it didn't kill them.

Chapter Seventeen

Sy waited in one of GreyFire's conference rooms. Erika, Jonathan, and four other GreyFire sentries sat around the rectangular table in the room with him. Since they had time to kill, he looked to Erika and asked, "Has anyone recognized the picture of the man who searched Howard's apartment?"

Erika shook her head. "No. I asked everyone who's ever had contact with Markgen, but the middle-aged man is a mystery."

He grunted. His brother's people hadn't seen him since, either, which made Sy think the bastard had fled. If neither DarkStalker nor GreyFire could find the human in the next few days, there would be little chance of ever finding him.

Of course, if they could find a way to beat this damn virus, the man would no longer be a threat.

When the sixth and last still healthy sentry came into the room and locked the door, Sy shifted his attention to the men and women in the room and said, "You're probably wondering why a cougar asked you to this meeting." There were a few mumbles and he continued. "The information in this room stays in this room. Are we clear?"

A man with tanned skin, dark brown eyes, and spiky black hair said, "I'm all for being civil, cougar, but you're a guest here, nothing more."

Sy raised an eyebrow and nodded at Erika. He didn't envy her task, but if she dreaded sharing the news, she didn't show it. Instead, her voice was full of dominance and authority when she said, "I'll allow that sign of disrespect only because of your ignorance, Tomás." She gestured toward Sylas. "Kaya declared a power share with Sylas Murray. With Kaya sick, he temporarily is our clan leader."

The room erupted with questions and Erika put up a hand. The voices died down and she said, "We don't want this news traveling around the clan. With the current sickness running rampant, this news might turn the den into chaos. Until we get Kaya better, I need all of you to work with Sy. Thanks to him, we might have a cure."

The man who'd spoken up before, Tomás, looked at him for a second. Then he said, "You're sleeping with Kaya again, aren't you?"

Sy growled. He was tired of people asking that fucking question; as if that was the only reason Kaya would ever ask for his help or rely on him.

Well, it was time to show them there was more to Sylas Murray than having Kaya for a girlfriend. "Enough. What is between Kaya and me is none of your damn business. Erika mentioned we might have a cure, so readjust your priorities or I'll find some other GreyFire members to help me. I was giving deference to your reputations, but so far they aren't matching up to the reality."

The room went silent. When one of the sentries spoke up, it wasn't Erika but rather Jonathan. He said, "Tell us what you know and what needs doing. Any feline who can sneak a punch on me definitely has my respect."

Sy nodded, grateful for the wolf's support. He recapped his interrogation with Kevin Howard and about the vial. Then he said, "The question is who do we risk as a guinea pig to see if Howard's vial works as promised? Kaya would want to use it on herself, but I know there are some wolves much sicker than her, so I wanted to hear your input. Especially since some of the sick wolves have already undergone cougar blood transfusions and I have no idea how that might affect the results." He looked at the woman at the far end of the table with short, blonde hair and green eyes. "Erika told me you have an M.D., Lisa. What's your medical opinion?"

The woman named Lisa placed her forearms on the table in front of her and said, "Well, if what Kevin said is true, and we have three doses available, I'd like to use one dose and split it to test for both adverse effects as well as to try to break down the compound so we can reproduce it. A few simple tests will let me know if the mixture of cougar-shifter and wolf-shifter blood will change the effectiveness of the cure."

"How long do you think that will take?"

Lisa shrugged. "For the transfusion-related test, probably the rest of today; as for the replication, a few days as long as my genius-level researcher, Donovan, remains healthy."

Sy nodded. "As soon as we're finished here, I want you to select a discreet team to carry out your ideas. And if this Donovan is as vital as you say, try to keep him away from any infected wolves for as long as possible."

Lisa said, "That shouldn't be a problem as he's not exactly a people person."

"Good." He looked around at the rest of the sentries. "After giving one dose to Lisa, that leaves two doses. Since Lisa's work will take some time, I still say we should offer a dose to one of the sick wolves. That way, if Lisa can replicate the formula, we'll know for sure that it'll work and we can start mass injecting everyone pronto."

Erika spoke up. "From what I've seen, the virus works faster on children than on adults. One of the infected children is faring pretty badly. He hasn't had a transfusion yet, so I can lay out the risks and ask his parents."

Sy wondered if Howard had ever thought about all the innocent children being hurt by his actions. But rather than waste his time thinking about that asshole, he said to Erika, "Do it." Then he looked at each and every face around the table. "As for the rest of you, I want you to keep your eyes and ears open. Keep track of where the virus is spreading and let me know straight away if you start showing symptoms." They all nodded and he said, "That's it for now. I need to call my brother and then go check on Kaya, unless you have any questions or concerns to report?"

No one replied, so he glanced to Erika, who shook her head.

The others remained quiet. He could tell they still hadn't warmed up to him, which was fine. For now.

All he cared about was Kaya and getting her clan healthy. If he could do that, then he would have plenty of time to warm up to the sentries. If not, well, he wasn't going to think about that. For Kaya's sake, he needed find a way to make it work.

Sy stood up. "Erika and Lisa, I hope you'll have news for me soon." He turned toward the door. "We'll reconvene this evening. I'll have Erika give you the time and place."

And with that, Sy left the room to go to Kaya. She had damned well better be still alive.

~~~

Kaya awoke from a dreamless sleep to find Sy sitting in a chair next to her bed with a laptop balanced on his legs. While she remembered waking up several times and falling back to sleep, her head was less fuzzy than the last time she'd been conscious.

And she was a whole hell of a lot less hot.

She tried to sit up, but her body was heavy, as if she had pushed her muscles to the breaking point by running thirty miles yesterday with a stone-filled backpack. Her feeble attempts to sit up caught Sy's eye, and he closed the laptop, tossed it aside, and leaned forward to cup her face with his hands. The instant he touched her skin, his eyes burned bright with happiness. "Kaya-love, your fever's broken."

She didn't have a fever? It took her a second for her cobweb-filled brain to process that, and then she said, "Tell me what happened, Sylas. Am I going to live?"

He stroked her cheeks with his thumbs. The action awoke her wolf, who had been too weak to make her presence known. Sy said, "Are you sure you're up for it? You've got to be exhausted right now."

Her inner wolf gave a weak growl. Kaya frowned and said, "Exhausted or not, tell me what the hell happened or I'll find someone else to give me the information."

He shook his head. "I think my question of whether your stubbornness would ever fade has been answered."

Before she could reply, he gave her a gentle kiss and said, "But I love your stubbornness, Kaya Alexie, so don't ever change."

Her irritation faded as quickly as it had come. "Tell me, Sy. Do I still have a clan to lead?"

His face became serious, and her heart skipped a beat. Had GreyFire been decimated? But if so, why had her fever broken?

She was about to demand an answer again, but Sy brushed the hair off her forehead and said, "Yes, Kaya, you have a clan. A few died before Donovan could manufacture a cure, but considering what could've happened, things are good."

Kaya closed her eyes. Most of her clan was still alive.

The momentary joy faded as she realized that while they were alive, they may no longer want her as their leader. After all, she hadn't recognized Kevin Howard as the threat he was, and on top of that, she'd put a cougar-shifter in charge while she'd lain sick.

But despite the fact she might lose her position, she was still happy GreyFire had survived and could better prepare against biological warfare in the future. It was time to put their medical research skills to use for more than financial gain. GreyFire might even extend a hand to some of the other shifter clans to work together.

Even if she were no longer their leader, she'd still do whatever it took to protect them. If that meant badgering their new leader with her ideas, so be it. If they kicked her out of the clan, she still had Sylas and he would help her with whatever stubborn proposals she came up with.

Still, she hoped that they didn't kick her out. Her heart ached at the idea.

She took a deep breath to clear the worry away so she could ask more questions. Neither Kaya nor her wolf liked the unknowing, even if it would hurt them in the long run.

She opened her eyes, looked back at Sylas, and said, "So how did you manage a cure?"

Sy continued to stroke her forehead, and she leaned into his touch. His voice only soothed her further as he explained about questioning Kevin Howard, finding his vial stash, and the ensuing race against the clock to test out and replicate the cure. They hadn't been able to find the person responsible on the Markgen side, but Sy didn't seem too worried about that since they now had a way to stop the deadly virus.

Kaya felt her energy waning. As happy as she was to find out everything that had happened, there was one more thing she needed to say before trying to get some rest. "Thank you, Sylas Murray, for taking care of my clan. I don't know what I would've done without you and your brother's help."

Sy's hand stilled on her head and she wondered what was wrong. Had he hated taking over GreyFire? Did he resent her for it? Had her wolves disrespected him the whole time?

But then he gave a lopsided smile and her worries eased. "You're welcome. But if you really want to thank me, get well soon so I can hand the damn wolves back over into your care."

Her wolf's protective instinct came to the forefront. "Did they mistreat you? If they did and they still keep me as their leader, so help me, they will get an earful."

He grinned. "Good to know they'd make your shit list. I wouldn't want to be on it." She frowned and he laughed before he said, "They were less than happy about it in the beginning, but once Jonathan of all people started back me up, the others soon followed suit. Tomás in particular was one difficult bastard to win over."

"That doesn't surprise me. His brother was killed by a snow leopard-shifter in Russia a few years back, and he holds it against all feline-shifters."

"Well, shit. You think Erika might've mentioned that to me."

Kaya had enough energy to muster a smile. "We need to keep you on your toes."

Sy leaned down and gently kissed her before he moved away and said, "You're looking tired, love. Why don't you sleep and we can talk more later?"

She knew he was right, but she fought off her tiredness. She wanted a few more minutes with her cougar-shifter. After contracting the virus, she had a whole new outlook on seizing what was important and never letting go.

And Sylas Murray was definitely something she wanted to keep close.

Rather than tell him how much she cared for him, she focused back on her clan and her own immediate future. She said, "I'll rest soon, but Sylas? Do you think the clan will want you to transfer the power back to me?"

He frowned. "Why wouldn't they? Have you not seen how they redecorated your room? If you think that's a 'fuck off' message, then I'm a bear-shifter."

He gestured around the room and for the first time she noticed the myriads of cards and handmade crafts covering the walls and every available inch of the tables and shelves in the room. Some cards were drawn with crayon, while others looked to be printed from a computer. From all those legible from her bed, they all asked for her to get well soon. Except for one extra-large card drawn with a purple crayon that had what she assumed was a wolf and cougar side-by-side with hearts drawn around it and the word 'LOVE' scrawled across the top in big letters.

Kaya blinked back tears. She tried not to get her hopes up, but she was pretty sure her clan still wanted her.

Sy took one of her hands and brought to his lips. "They're waiting for your Kaya, just as I am."

If it were anyone else with her in this room, she'd hold back her tears and put on a brave face. But this was Sylas, her cougar-shifter and future mate, and she would never hide anything from him. Ever.

A tear rolled down her cheek. Sy wiped it away and said, "What's wrong, love? Tell me."

She gave a rather undignified sniffle. "Don't worry; I'm just happy."

He kissed her hand again and said, "If you're happy now, just wait until you're better."

"What are you talking about?"

He grinned, a twinkle in his eye. "You'll see." She opened her mouth, but Sy shook his head and said, "No. Get some rest, love. I want you to get your strength back as soon as possible. In addition to my surprise, I want to call in my favors to devour you in my bed. The sooner the better."

While her body was too weak for sex right now, his promise brought forth images in her mind of them naked and tangled in her bed.

Sylas naked and hers? That sounded like a perfect future. "I look forward to it, my mate-to-be. I have a few tricks I want to try with you while we're both naked."

She'd said the words "mate-to-be" casually to test out the waters, but Sy's grin told her everything she needed to know about whether his feelings remained the same as before. He said, "You haven't technically asked me, oh, great clan leader. Shifter tradition requires the clan leader to ask for a mating, but when you're ready, I'm pretty sure I'll say yes."

At the laughter in his eyes, Kaya wanted to throw a pillow at him. However, since that would take too much energy, she said, "Give me a kiss and then go annoy someone else for a while."

He laughed. Then he leaned down and gave her a slow, lingering kiss. Her breath had to be awful, but judging by the way his tongue swept into her mouth in a sign of possession, he didn't seem to mind.

It made her love him all the more.

Sy broke the kiss and stroked her hair. "Get well, Kaya. We have two weeks until the celebration with the DarkStalker cougars, so get your ass well by then."

She wanted to ask about the celebration, but it was getting harder and harder to keep her eyes open. Part of the reason she'd won the clan vote to be leader three years ago was because she accepted her limitations rather than tried to hide them. Well, most of the time, anyway.

This was one of those times, so she nodded and said, "Sounds good."

Sy stood up and started humming an old shifter tune, one used to lull children to sleep. It was ridiculous for him to use it on her, a grown adult, but she learned something new about him—Sy could sing, and his voice was warm and soothing. Before she was aware of what was happening, she drifted off into unconsciousness.

Chapter Eighteen

Two weeks later, Kaya was in her office filling out some paperwork to solidify the new terms with Markgen. Since working with another company meant starting the clinical trials all over again, which would lose them both a lot of money, she'd given Markgen's CEO a list of demands that needed to be met in order for her to stay and continue the trials. While not happy about working with the company, at least they were doing a thorough investigation into what had happened. Markgen's CEO had assured her that any employee who had helped Dr. Smith would be turned over to the authorities.

Her wolf thought that was too light a sentence, but Kaya was doing the best she could for her clans' survival.

There was a knock on her door and she pushed her paperwork to the side. She wasn't expecting anyone, but her pack was just starting to recover from the sickness and loss and they knew she was always available. "Come in."

Sy peeked his head into her office and her wolf, who had been dozing while she'd done the tedious human stuff, perked up. They had both missed him, even if they'd seen him only a few hours ago.

Sy raised his brows and said, "Is there anything you absolutely must get done before tonight, or can you spare the next two hours?"

Reclaiming the Wolf

She had a feeling she knew what he was asking. After all, her doctor had only cleared her for good health this morning.

Which meant she was allowed to have sex again.

Not that having Sylas Murray spooned around her at night for the last two weeks hadn't been fabulous, but she'd missed his hands caressing her skin, his tongue lapping between her legs, and, of course, his cock pounding into her from behind.

Remembering the last time he'd done those three things, her wolf urged her to stop with the human stuff and go to their cougar. They needed his touch. He would make them feel better.

Yes, but let's make him work for it. The wolf sulked, but understood she wanted to play with their soon-to-be-mate.

She shook her head and said, "No, I don't have anything that can't wait. Come in and tell me what's up."

Grinning, Sy stepped into her office. As she always did when she saw him, she gave his tall, muscled body a sweep with her eyes, but she stopped at his t-shirt and burst out laughing.

Sylas Murray, badass cougar-shifter extraordinaire, was wearing an "I Heart Wolves" t-shirt.

She finally got her laughter under control and said, "I'm surprised you wore that thing voluntarily. We haven't had a chance to do our rematch, which means you never lost our bet."

Sy shrugged. "Wearing an 'I Heart Wolves' t-shirt has brought some smiles and laughter. I figured what the hell. It would probably help the clan with both their sadness from the last few weeks as well as help ease the clan's nerves about this afternoon's celebration."

Some of her good cheer faded, but not all. The ten deaths from the virus had hit GreyFire hard. The clan was starting to recover and get back on their feet, but it would take some time. In another week, she could probably tell Kian that his cougar-shifters could go back home.

Well, except for Sylas, of course. She was keeping him.

She smiled and said, "The celebration will go fine. I don't know what the hell they're so worried about, especially after everything the cougars did to help us." She leaned forward on her desk and raised an eyebrow. "So, tell me why your sexy self is in my office?"

Light danced in his eyes. "Now that you're well, I can finally give you my surprise."

"You mean the one you've been taunting me with for the past two weeks?"

He grinned. "That's the one."

He walked over to her desk and sat on the edge. Then he took a folded piece of paper out of his pocket and handed it to her. "Ta-da, here it is."

She took the rumpled piece of paper that looked as if he'd been carrying it around in his pocket for some time. As she unfolded it, she glanced up at him and said, "There had better be something pretty damn fantastic on this piece of paper to merit all of your hinting about it."

He made a motion with his hand for her to look at it. She glanced down and saw it was a letter. Curious to see what it said, she read it:

Dearest Kaya:

I've spent the last few weeks, or should I say, years, trying to find a word to describe how sorry I am for abandoning you at our mating ceremony ten years ago. But one doesn't exist. I was a coward, plain and simple. Your uncle threatened to attack Clan DarkStalker if I went through with our mating, and rather than consult you and my clan leader for help, I took the out to join the army.

Reclaiming the Wolf

Not that I'm trying to pass the blame on to your uncle. Ultimately, it was my choices that hurt you. I can't even imagine what it must've been like for you to stand alone among a clan of wolf-shifters who had warned you against me from the beginning. Their smugness alone must've crushed your heart.

But all of that is in the past and as much as I might want to, I can't change it. Instead, what I can do is focus on the future.

If you would take a chance on me and allow me to have your heart again, I will never, ever abandon you. I tried to show you how much I wanted to make this work by managing our clan—yes, our clan—to the best of my ability while you were sick. This may not be enough to convince you that I mean to stay forever this time, no matter what challenges we face, but I will do whatever it takes, Kaya, because I love you and I want to spend the rest of my life with you.

Love,

Sylas Horatio Murray

Her heart was now pounding inside her chest. Sylas wanted to stay with her forever.

Kaya blinked back the tears that threatened to fall and looked up into Sy's eyes. The look there was vulnerable. The fact that the cocky, self-assured cougar-shifter was nervous made her soften even more.

She had a feeling he'd written the letter to give her a taste of what he'd sent before, a decade ago. But her disappointment and heartbreak concerning the cougar-shifter was in the past. Kaya, too, could only focus on the future.

And she knew what she wanted.

She stood up and walked around her desk to stand between Sy's legs. She looped her hands around his neck and stared him dead in the eye. She had a question she needed to ask. "Sylas

Horatio Murray, will you do me the honor of becoming my mate?"

His eyes flashed to a deeper cougar green and back before he growled, "Yes" and took her lips in a possessive kiss.

~~~

Every muscle in Sy's body tensed as he watched Kaya read his letter. He'd written dozens of drafts, but he'd decided that this was the best he could do while still remaining himself. He only hoped she agreed.

As the seconds ticked by, Sy tried to think of how else he could prove he wouldn't abandon her ever again when Kaya looked up.

And the woman looked about ready to cry.

His cougar growled, not liking to see their wolf upset. But as she stood up and walked over to stand in between his legs, hope surged in his heart. Maybe her tears were of joy and not because his letter had brought up their rocky past.

Kaya looped her arms around his neck and it took everything he had not to pull her close for a kiss. This was too important. He needed to know how she responded.

She ran her fingers along the back of his neck and said, "Sylas Horatio Murray, will you do me the honor of becoming my mate?"

Time stilled for a second as he processed her words. Despite everything that happened, she still wanted him.

Joy surged through his body and he wanted—no, needed—to kiss her. He whispered, "Yes," before lowering his head for a kiss.

He didn't try to be gentle. With Kaya healthy, it was time to release the rougher side of him.

Sy thrust his tongue into her mouth. As he twined his tongue with hers, she fisted his hair. Suddenly, kissing her wasn't enough and he hauled her body up against his, the softness of her breasts and the sharp points of her nipples making his cock as hard as steel.

Claim her. She is ours, his cougar growled.

Sy agreed. He broke their kiss, nipped Kaya's bottom lip, and said, "Take off your shirt."

There were times to tease and dawdle, but this was not one of them and Kaya understood that. She lifted her shirt over her head as he tore off his own.

He ran his hands up her ribcage, over her beautiful bronze skin, and traced the edge of her black and white bra. He'd have to ask her to wear this one again. It somehow managed to both highlighted her strength while also making her extremely feminine.

That fit his wolf to a T.

For now, however, he wanted to see more of her. He pulled down the cups of her bra to expose her high, small breasts. Her dark nipples were already hard, and he tugged each of them in turn.

Kaya sucked in a breath and he looked up into her eyes. "Are you wet for me, love? Or do you need some more encouragement?"

"I'm always wet for you, Sylas. Now take off your pants."

He smiled at her bossy tone. He smacked her ass and pushed her away so he could shed the rest of his clothes.

By the time he'd shucked his shoes, socks, and pants—he'd been optimistic and gone commando—Kaya was standing naked and rolling one of her nipples between her thumb and forefinger, a sexy smile on her face.

Take her.

Sy didn't need any more encouragement. He stalked over to Kaya and backed her against the wall. She put her hands on his chest, but he took her wrists and pinned them over her head.

Her breath was hot on his chin as she leaned her hips against his cock. Sy kept her hands pinned with one hand and moved a hand down her smooth stomach until he reached between her legs. As he ran his fingers through her folds, he growled at how wet she was.

Kaya murmured, "Is that the best you can do?"

He'd planned on fucking her with his tongue, but at her goading, he took her hard little clit between his fingers and pinched. Hard.

Kaya moaned and arched her back. He could tell she wanted more, but he released her clit and nuzzled her neck. "I see you didn't learn anything back in the cave." He nipped her neck and licked his bite with his tongue. "I think it's time to show you once and for all that your pussy belongs to me and only me."

~~~

Kaya had thought she'd been wet before, then Sy had told her that her pussy belonged to him; she now felt her juices coating her inner thighs.

She wanted this desperately, but knew that begging would only turn Sy off. He liked her strong for a reason.

So she said, "Fuck me hard enough and I may just agree with you."

190

RECLAIMING THE WOLF

Sy growled and moved his free arm under her ass and lifted her as if she weighed no more than a feather. In response, she wrapped her long legs around Sy's trim waist. And now, with her pussy a few inches from his cock, he released her hands to wrap his other arm around her ribcage and said, "Position me so I can fuck you against the wall."

After two weeks of celibacy, she didn't need to be told twice. She gripped his hard, long cock and maintained eye contact as she gave him a squeeze. "Tell me your dick belongs to me, and I'll consider it."

"It always has, Kaya-love, and it always will."

Love surged through her body and her wolf howled. *He is ours.*

She positioned him and he thrust to the hilt. She gripped his shoulders and extended her claws a fraction. He hissed as the sharp tips broke his skin, but then he growled and started pounding in and out, each thrust forcing her harder against the wall. She might have bruises tomorrow, but as his long, hard cock started hitting her g-spot, waves of pleasure coursed through her body with each thrust.

She moaned and decided that bruises would be totally worth it.

He moved his arm from around her ribcage so that her back was now against the wall, giving him more leverage to pound into her. He fisted a hand into her hair and pulled her in for a kiss. Without preamble, his tongue swept into her mouth and their teeth clashed. He wasn't so much kissing her as dominating her.

But damn, the man knew how to kiss.

He simultaneously released her hair and her mouth and she cried out at the loss. But then, he moved a hand between them to rub her clit, and Kaya tilted her head against the wall behind her. "Fuck yes."

Sy growled and thrust even faster, his balls now slapping against the lower part of her ass. The pressure was building and Kaya clung to his shoulders and leaned forward to kiss him. This time, she swept into his mouth and explored every inch, wanting to memorize every contour and crevice of him.

Then Sy pinched her clit and she cried out as her orgasm hit her, the waves of pleasure and pain almost too much to handle.

As her pussy clenched and released around his cock, Sy broke their kiss and bit her shoulder as he stilled and came inside her.

They remained like that for about a minute. Then he released her shoulder and laid his forehead against her neck. His breath was hot against her skin and she moved one of her hands to his hair. As she gently pet him, he started to give the human equivalent of a purr. His voice was deep and husky when he said, "So who owns your pussy?"

"You."

He kissed her neck and raised his head. The look in his eyes was possessive and fierce. "You hesitated a second. I think you need more convincing."

She truly didn't, but she lived to tease her cougar-shifter. "The woman might be convinced, but the wolf needs more."

He ran his hands up along her ribcage to under her arms. Then he stepped back from the wall and lowered her, his cock sliding out of her along the way.

Neither she nor her wolf liked the sudden empty feeling.

Sy released her and motioned to the ground. "Then get down and show me your beautiful ass so I can take you from behind."

She might've just orgasmed, but her clit was already throbbing again in anticipation.

Still, she couldn't resist reaching out and squeezing Sy's cock. Coated in her juices, she easily pulled up and down his length and some of Sy's determined glint turned into desire. "Ask nicely, Sylas."

He moved to take her shoulders, but Kaya released his dick and stepped back. She raised an eyebrow, knowing full well she'd pay for it.

That thought only made her hotter.

"Please, Kaya, get on all fours so I can fuck your wolf into submission."

Do it, her wolf urged. She was impatient. She'd let them do it the human way. She wanted the wolf way.

Kaya strode to the far side of the room so that Sy would follow the sway of her ass with his eyes. In a clear space on the floor, she kneeled down before lowering herself to all fours. She wiggled her ass in the air. To prod him even further, she said, "Hurry up before I change my mind."

Sy growled. A few seconds later, she felt his heat behind her and without a word he thrust into her.

Kaya moaned as he started his rough assault all over again. Sylas Murray definitely owned her pussy, and she loved every hard, long stroke of it.

CHAPTER NINETEEN

Three hours later, Sylas was once again dressed in his "I Heart Wolves" t-shirt, his arm around his mate-to-be as they walked through the forest to where the dual clan celebration was being held. Kaya had tried to convince him to change, but he'd said no. He didn't want there to be any doubt of where his heart belonged.

Of course, looking over at his sexy wolf, he wished they could both be naked again. She was wearing a dark blue dress that hugged her breasts before flaring out, the skirt stopping just above her knee. His cougar wanted her to cover up those gorgeous legs from the other males, but Sy told his cat to settle down. She was theirs.

And they would make it official this evening.

But Sy was getting ahead of himself. They were going to meet with his brother and his mate first. The consensus had been to let the gathering start without the clan leaders. Not that they were letting it be a free-for-all; the seconds from each clan were keeping an eye on things in case they turned south. Especially since alcohol was being provided.

They were nearly to the meeting point. Since they were early, Sy hugged Kaya close to his side and kissed the top of her head. "Are you sure we can't disappear into the woods for half an hour? I'm sure your wolf would like it if I took you out in the open."

Kaya looked up at him with a slight frown on her face. "You might've forgotten, but my lady parts are out of practice and need a little time to recover. As it is, I think I'm going to have bruises along my back, not to mention the scratches on the side of my hips."

He squeezed her hip, careful to avoid where she was tender from his claws earlier. "Hey, you can't blame me. I just gave my lady what she wanted. Next time, I can be all delicate and barely touch you if that'll make you happier."

She full-on frowned. "Do that and I'll leave your ass for another male."

He growled, pulled them to a stop and brought Kaya flush against his front. "Never."

She started to pet his chest with long, slow strokes. "Calm down, kitty cat. I was just teasing."

He gave her a quick kiss before letting her go so they could start walking again. "Come on, let's keep going. My sister-in-law is going to be smug as hell, and I want to get it over with as soon as possible."

~~~

Kaya didn't hold back her grin at that. She was looking forward to meeting face-to-face with Trinity and Kian when her clan wasn't on the brink of collapse.

She leaned into Sy's side and wish she could just disappear into the woods with her cougar. Despite her earlier protests, she could take more sex, a lot more.

But this was one of those times when being clan leader meant putting your own needs second. Ensuring the truce not only continued with DarkStalker, but strengthened, was necessary for her clan's survival.

Besides, she owed Kian and his cougars the life of her clan. This was just the first step in repaying that debt.

They reached the clearing with a high rock formation to one side. It was near the border between DarkStalker's and GreyFire's land, the same place where Sy had cheated eleven years ago to get her naked under the stars. In that second, she realized that neither one of them had actually touched the rock all those years ago.

Let's win, her wolf urged, and Kaya agreed.

Before Sy could get the same idea, Kaya broke free of his arm and raced to the rock. She slapped her hand against the cool, smooth surface and grinned at her cougar-shifter. "I win."

He frowned. "Since when was there a competition?"

She pointed a finger at him. "Technically, neither of us won that night you told me you loved me for the first time. You never touched the rock. You only tackled me to the ground. It may have taken eleven years to complete, but I just won our game."

Sy studied her for a second and then gave her a heated a look as he stalked to her. When he was directly in front of her, he caged her body with his arms against the rock behind her. "And what do you want to claim as your prize, Kaya-love?"

It was hard to think of anything as his heat and scent surrounded her, but then she remembered his brother should be here any minute. She wasn't a prude, but she'd rather not have her soon to be brother-in-law catch her in the act of having sex with Sylas.

Reclaiming the Wolf

She may not be able to get her male naked right now, but she needed to touch him. She placed her hands on Sy's chest and started to stroke, wishing it was the hair of his chest under her fingers instead of his t-shirt. She looked up to meet his eyes. There was only one thing she wanted, so she simply said, "I want you."

He leaned down to nuzzle her cheek. "You already have me, love. Try again."

She ran her hands up his chest and then to the back of his neck. There was one other thing this strong, sexy male could give her.

She whispered into his ear and said, "Once everything is settled down and GreyFire is back to normal, you can try giving me some pups."

He dropped his hands and hauled her body up against his. She squeaked in surprise, but Sy paid no attention as he whispered, "Maybe a cub and a pup. I'm already outnumbered and I need some support of the feline variety to remain sane."

She smiled. The image of a little cougar cub and a wolf pup chasing each other around her and Sylas came into her head and a deep yearning rushed forth. She'd never thought much of having children before, but she'd love nothing more if it was with the man currently holding her close. True, they might turn out to be the most stubborn shifter children on the planet, but she had a feeling they could handle them.

Wanting to tease him again, she cupped his face and moved his head so she could look into his eyes. "Well, I think whether we have pups or cubs depends on whose DNA is more dominant and stubborn. Personally, I'm betting on mine."

Sy laughed before he took her mouth in a demanding kiss. Kaya was so lost in his taste and the feel of him that she nearly jumped when she heard a female voice say, "Hello, lovebirds. Care to make yourself decent?"

Sy, on the other hand, took his time to finish caressing the inside of her mouth before pulling away and turning them both around to face Kian and Trinity.

Trinity was grinning while Kian looked amused. They both walked toward them, Kian limping a little due to his old injury.

Not that she held that against him. The man might be smiling, but there was an aura of power around him. Her wolf wasn't about to cower, but it recognized an equal when she saw one.

Of course, when Trinity leaned against her mate, he softened and her wolf approved.

Kaya tried to move to greet their guests, but Sy kept his arm around her waist. She pinched his arm and said, "Let me go." His grip tightened. She sighed and said, "Look, I know your cougar is tetchy right now, until the mating ceremony finishes, but it's your brother. I hardly think Trinity is going to allow him to rip off my clothes or attack me."

~~~

Sy ignored Kaya's pinch and squeezed her closer. The human part of him understood her reasoning, but his cougar didn't. Until everyone knew she was their female, they needed to keep her close.

Calm down, kitty cat. His inner cougar growled at that, but his jealousy eased a fraction. Still, Sy wasn't about to take chances. "He's still another male. My cat doesn't like that."

"Sylas." He looked up at his brother's authoritative tone and Kian continued. "Take some advice from me, brother. Learn to let her go every once in a while or there'll be hell to pay later."

Trinity glared in her mate's direction. "Care to explain that one, mister?"

Kian shrugged. "Whenever I act too overprotective, you withhold sex. I'm trying to save my brother some heartache. Strong women take a special kind of touch." Kian nuzzled the side of Trin's head. "And I wouldn't have it any other way."

Trinity battled a frown, but Sy could tell his sister-in-law was softening. Then she looked to Kaya and he knew she was about to cause trouble. Trin said, "If it weren't for the mating ceremony, I'd suggest that we ditch these two alphas and let them stew a bit."

Sy looked down to see Kaya grinning. Yes, Trinity Perez-Murray was going to be a bad influence on his soon-to-be mate.

His wolf-shifter said, "Next time. If Kian is anything like his brother, I'm sure there'll be plenty of opportunities for us to let them stew."

Trin laughed and Sy decided he needed to change topics. While he was glad the two women were getting along, he didn't want to give Trin more time to influence Kaya. Kian's mate was headstrong and full of ideas, ideas that Kaya would like a little too much.

Determined to move things along, he said, "Are you two done conspiring against me and my brother? I want to get to the celebration and stake my claim."

Kaya wrapped an arm around his waist and squeezed. The touch made his cougar purr. Looking up at him, she said, "I thought I was the one staking the claim. Shifter tradition dictates it's up to the clan leader."

He huffed. "I don't care who does the claiming. I just want it done."

Kaya laughed. "Okay, Mr. Grumpy." She looked toward Kian. "Do you think our clan members have had enough time to try and bond, at least a little?"

Kian grinned with a glint of mischief in his eye. "We took a peek on our way here, and things are interesting, to say the least."

Trinity shook her head. "He means the guys are punching each other."

He felt Kaya tense beside him. "What? Did you stop them?"

Kian said, "No. It wasn't a bad kind of fighting. Sometimes male shifters need a punch or two to accept each other."

Sy chuckled and Kaya glared up at him. He explained, "The same thing happened with Jonathon. In the end, he backed me up because I was able to sneak a punch on him." He shrugged. "But maybe we should go before it turns into something less friendly."

Kaya gave him a look. "I think you're using them as an excuse to get the mating ceremony over quicker."

He grinned, seeing no point in hiding it. "But of course."

Kaya sighed, and then looked to Kian. "Is that okay? We can have a real meeting later."

Kian shrugged. "No problem. I'm pretty anxious myself to see my brother settled down. I was starting to think it'd never happen and I'd have to put up with him for the next fifty years."

Sy rolled his eyes. "Gee, thanks, brother. I'm feeling the love big time."

Kian grinned. "Hey, once you're mated, then we can discuss our women, just like they'll discuss us. Being shackled works both ways, after all."

Trinity poked him in the side. "Yes, shackled. I'll remember that." Trin smiled at Sy and Kaya. "Let's go, lovebirds."

His brother and Trinity turned and started walking. Kaya moved to go, but he couldn't resist keeping her close long enough to whisper, "Shackles. Now there's an idea."

"Sylas."

He laughed at her reprimand. "Come on. We can experiment with our kinky honeymoon period later. Let's go see how the two clans are faring."

~~~

When they finally entered the large clearing being used for the ceremony, Kaya did a sweep with her eyes. There was a large group of her wolves to one side, in a mixture of human and wolf forms. Ditto for the cougars in a different section of the space, but what caught her eye was the large gathering of males and females from both clans standing around two males, shouting and cheering.

At her side, Sy said, "Looks like Aidan is taking on Tomás."

She'd vaguely recognized the cougar-shifter and she now remembered where she'd seen him—Aidan had been with Sylas when they'd first shown up on her land with the dead wolf-shifter.

While Aidan was taller with a long, lean build, he was also older, maybe forty. Tomás was stocky and in as stellar shape as the cougar, but he was in his late twenties. Their advantages and disadvantages seemed to be balancing each other because whenever Aidan managed to get a hold on Tomás, the younger man was able to slip away. Then when Tomás went for a punch to the kidney, Aidan anticipated it and merely sidestepped.

Since the two males were already covered in sweat, Kaya reckoned they had been at this for a while. She gently nudged Sy's side. "Do you think it'll be over soon? If not, I'm going to call it off."

Sy squeezed her side. "Give it a second and...there you go."

Aidan finally managed to get a grip on the wolf and pin him face down to the ground. Due to the combination of the older shifter's height, weight, and experienced grip, Tomás would have no choice to cede defeat.

Her wolf was anxious and curious at the same time. Would the men keep fighting? Would everyone go back to their respective clan groups?

Tomás said something she couldn't hear and Aidan grinned. When he rose and offered a hand to the younger man, he took it and Kaya relaxed. She relaxed further when various males and females started congratulating Aidan. One female in particular, one of her wolves, was all but rubbing against the cougar-shifter male.

Kaya gave a low snort. "Well, I think that answers my question about the two clans ever getting along. Your hotties are already attracting some of my women and probably some of my men, too."

Sy growled. "Hotties? You think Aidan is attractive?"

Normally, she'd tease Sy, but she could tell he was on edge at the moment, so she put a hand on his chest and stroked. "You're my hottie, Sylas. Now, let's go make it official before another fight starts."

Sy's tension eased and Kaya resisted making a remark about male shifter egos.

RECLAIMING THE WOLF

As they made their way to the makeshift dais near the bar and refreshments, Kaya's heart rate ticked up. This was it. She was about to be mated.

She wasn't nervous about her choice of mate. There would never be anyone but Sylas Murray for her. But still, she was worried about her clan. They seemed to like him well enough, but this would be the true test since the ceremony required some of their participation.

Memories of everyone turning their back on her during the last time she'd wanted to pledge herself to Sylas came flooding back, but she forced them aside. Things were different this time. Sy wasn't going to run, and he'd proven himself with at least some of her clan. Surely someone would stand up and second the mating.

As if sensing her unease, Sy leaned down to her ear and whispered, "It'll be fine, love. Not everyone likes me, but enough do that the rest should at least learn to tolerate me with time. Besides, if we feline hotties are attracting your men and women, then everyone is just going to have to get used to this kind of thing."

Sy using the word "hottie" made Kaya laugh and her nervousness eased. Sy always seemed able to do that.

"Well, I don't know about your feline females, but you male cougars are in for a surprise when it comes to wolf females. We're a lot to handle and aren't afraid to bite."

He grinned. "You say that as if it's a bad thing."

They made it to the dais, ascended the stairs, and Kaya laced her fingers of one hand through Sylas's as she faced out. People were still far flung across the clearing, so she gave a high-pitched whistle. The clearing slowly silenced and when Kian and

Trinity moved to stand in front of them below, everyone else start to follow suit.

When most everyone was in front of them, Sy squeezed her hand and she squeezed back.

Despite the pounding of her heart, Kaya kept a calm face, stood tall, and said in a booming voice, "While we're here to celebrate the growing friendship between our two clans, we're also here to celebrate something else. I didn't mention it earlier because I didn't know this would happen until just a few hours ago, but we're going to have a mating ceremony."

A murmur went through the crowd. Kaya raised her free hand up to signal silence, and most of the murmuring died down. She continued, "I'm not sure how much Kian has told DarkStalker about recent events, but you all are aware of the virus that nearly destroyed GreyFire. I, myself, fell sick and proclaimed a power share with Sylas Murray. He took charge and did everything he could to save my clan. Without his help, we may never have found a cure. He has proven himself a worthy male, and what's more, I love him." Sy squeezed her hand again and Kaya pushed on. "So I ask for your respect and cooperation to allow this mating ceremony to go forward."

Kaya fell silent and waited. Someone needed to give their blessing and be seconded before she could move on. Thankfully, Kian's voice boomed over the clearing. "As leader of Clan DarkStalker, you have my blessing. You make my brother happy. I can ask for no better sister-in-law."

Kian's words went straight to her heart. To be first meant he truly accepted her.

She nodded at the other leader and then looked out to the crowd. She was only halfway there. "Will anyone second this mating?"

Erika Washington raised a hand and said, "I second it. Sylas Murray has earned my respect, and what's more, he makes you happy. We'll just make sure to hide the ribbons and string from the kitty cat."

Most of the shifters in the crowd, from both clans, laughed and Kaya could feel the tension easing.

She nodded. "Then with a seconded approval, I'll proceed."

She turned toward Sy and reluctantly released his hand. She raised one hand palm up and said, "You've earned my love, my trust, and my respect." She raised her other hand and extended a claw on her forefinger before swiping it across her palm. As blood welled, she said, "By joining our blood together, we will become mates in all things—as friends, equals, lovers, and one day, I hope, parents. If you accept my claim, let our blood mingle as one to seal the bond."

While she remained calm on the outside, she let her love and yearning show in her eyes. Sy's eyes flashed a bright cougar green before he raised his palm and sliced his skin. As the blood welled, he said, "I love you, Kaya Alexie, and would love nothing more than to be your mate." He turned his cut palm onto hers and squeezed. With a twinkle in his eyes, he said, "And it's about damn time too."

The crowd laughed, but Kaya barely heard them as she stared into Sy's eyes. While he'd held her heart for a long time, he was now officially hers.

She tilted her head and Sy leaned down to kiss her. As she melted into her mate's touch, both Kaya and her inner wolf felt complete for the first time in their lives. With Sylas at her side, she could face anything.

Dear Reader:

Would you like to know when my next release is available? (And receive exclusive goodies and information too?) You can sign up for my newsletter at www.jessiedonovan.com or by liking my Facebook page at http://www.facebook.com/JessieDonovanAuthor.

Also, I need to ask you a favor. Word-of-mouth is crucial for any author to succeed. If you enjoyed this book, please consider leaving a review. Even if it's only a line or two, it would be a huge help!

I've included a short excerpt from the next Cascade Shifters story (*Cougar's First Christmas*, #1.5). You might also enjoy the first installment of my dragon-shifter serial series, *Sacrificed to the Dragon*, or the first book in my Asylums for Magical Threats paranormal romance series, *Blaze of Secrets*. Turn the page for a glimpse of my other works.

With Gratitude,
Jessie Donovan

Check out the next Cascade Shifter story…Excerpt from
Cougar's First Christmas **(CS #1.5)**

CHAPTER ONE

Sean Fisher was putting the last few sprinkles on his slightly burnt, reindeer-shaped sugar cookies when his cell phone went off. He looked at the screen, saw it was his older sister, Danika, and clicked receive. "Hey, kitty cat, what's up?"

His sister growled over the line. "I'll make sure to call you kitten every chance I get if you ever let me meet your human girlfriend."

Sean glanced at the clock. "Introducing Lauren to a group of cougar-shifters is bad enough. Introducing her to you is like a nightmare."

"Hey, if she can't stand up to me, she doesn't deserve my baby brother. The Fisher family protects its own."

Despite having heard his sister say that sentence ten thousand times before, he still smiled. "Is there a reason you're calling? I have special plans for my female tonight, and you're kind of taking away time from my awesome preparations."

"I'm calling because I just heard through the grapevine about you meeting the human's parents tomorrow. Are you sure that's a smart idea? If this isn't serious, Sean, then don't risk both yourself and this Lauren woman, especially since Human Purity is looking for targets in the Seattle area."

Of course his sister had heard about his plans. Danika Fisher kept the pulse of the clan to such a degree he wouldn't be surprised if she knew everyone's darkest secrets.

Still, her concerns about Human Purity were valid. They were a group of religious and secular protesters who believed humans and shifters should be segregated. "Look, Dani, I'm twenty-five years old and I can take care of myself. You're the one who trained me as a teenager, after all. So unless you doubt your own skills, trust me for once."

"It's not a matter of trusting you, Sean. They're starting to kidnap shifters and make videos showing their torture and killings. One cougar-shifter doesn't stand a chance against a gang from Purity armed with tranquilizers."

"Of course I know that, Dani, but meeting her family tomorrow is important. I love Lauren Spencer with every cell in my body, and I want her to be my mate."

He hadn't meant for that secret to come out, but there it was.

The line went silent for a few seconds. Then Dani said, "Matings and marriages between shifters and humans are illegal, little brother."

He turned away from the sugar cookies on the kitchen counter and clenched his free hand. "I don't care. She's mine, and if I have to wait ten years for the law to change in order to make it official, then so be it."

"If that's what you want, then go for it. Just don't expect me to be all sugary nice when I first meet her. If she runs from me, then she's not worth the trouble or possible jail time, Sean."

While he was ninety-eight percent sure Lauren would do just fine with his sister and his clan, he wasn't about to let his sister know there was any doubt at all. "We'll see if you don't end up running from her. After all, she knows the correct dosages to knock a shifter unconscious before she pulls out all your teeth."

His sister snorted. "Only you could make being a dental student sound scary."

Smiling, Sean glanced to the clock. "I really need to go, Dani. Lauren will be here any minute. I'll call you after the Winter Celebration."

"Just be extra careful, Sean. And give a growl in greeting to your female."

He gave his sister a growl. "I threw it back at you instead. Bye, Dani."

He tossed the phone aside. His sister's warnings were valid, but Lauren's parents only lived about an hour from Seattle, in a city called Lakewood. Since they would be on I-5, the major freeway, almost the entire time, they would be fine.

Pushing his sister's worries aside, he took one last look around his small apartment to make sure everything was ready. Presents were wrapped under his very first, and somewhat lopsided, Christmas tree. Lauren's fuzzy, red and white stocking, which held his most important gift, was atop the coffee table since he didn't have a fireplace. Lights danced around the ceiling, reflecting off the glass snowflakes he'd found today at the last minute. And finally, his sugar cookies, made from a box mix, were decorated and waiting.

To him, it looked more like a Christmas bomb had exploded inside his apartment, but Lauren would like it.

Over the last six months, his female had done so much to accept his shifter ways, such as accepting him in cat-form and allowing him to scent-mark her apartment. So this was his way of trying to accept her human traditions. After all, shifters didn't celebrate Christmas, but rather held a winter celebration instead.

Since he fully intended to have Lauren as his mate, he needed to prove to her that he could make her happy. Giving her a great Christmas, her favorite holiday, was only the start.

Meeting her family tomorrow was just as important since it would allow her to see what she was getting into. Lauren was close to her family, and it would tear her apart if they didn't accept him.

His inner cougar growled at his uncertainty. *It will be fine. She is ours. She is strong.*

Pacing the living room, he realized his cougar was right. Over the last six months, they'd faced death threats and censure everywhere they went. Hell, just being his girlfriend and spending the night at his apartment could get her arrested.

Lauren wasn't a weak human. No, she had a hidden strength that both man and cougar admired.

Still, he was nervous. If tomorrow didn't go well and her family rejected him, she might leave him.

Stop it, asshole. Everything would be fine. His little human loved him, and damn it, he would try his best to ensure they had a future together.

~~~

Lauren Spencer pulled into the parking lot of Sean's apartment building and turned off the ignition. Glancing at the rearview mirror, she waited to see if the blue sedan that had been tailing her from the university would pull in after her. She counted to sixty, but no other cars pulled into the lot. She brushed off the car as coincidence.

Being paranoid sucked big-time, but her choice of boyfriend made her the target of some very dangerous people, such as Human Purity. And Purity had a hatred of shifters unlike anything since the Nazi's hatred of the Jews in World War II.

Not that she would trade Sean for anything. Just thinking about her boyfriend in his beautiful tan-furred and blue-eyed cougar form as she stroked his back, or the way he loved to nuzzle her neck while in human form before he kissed her, warmed Lauren's heart. How her blabbing during his emergency visit to her dental school six months ago, and asking to see his feline teeth no less, had led to this point in her life, she didn't know. But she had no regrets, and tomorrow she looked forward to finally introducing Sean to her parents and brother.

Realizing tomorrow was Christmas Eve, Lauren's thoughts about Human Purity vanished, and she felt a rush of giddiness. Ever since she'd been a child, Lauren had loved Christmas. Not because of receiving presents or stuffing her face at Christmas dinner, but because of the gathering of the family and all of their crazy traditions. No doubt her mother would have the same fifteen different types of cookies she made every year stashed in the freezer, off limits to everyone until Christmas Day. Not even her shifter boyfriend would be able to sneak one past her mother's careful watch.

She only hoped her mother liked Sean. If he were human, she'd be fine with it even though Sean was white and she was black, but shifters were a whole other group. Not everyone approved of their animal sides and believed them little better than beasts to be tamed.

Stop it, Lauren. Mom will love him like you do. Holding that thought close, Lauren exited the car with her duffel bag in hand, ascended the stairs to Sean's third floor apartment, and knocked.

A small part of her wished she had a key, but a key to a shifter's apartment could land her in jail. After all, they weren't legally supposed to live together. Some cops would look the other way, but Sean hadn't wanted to risk it. As such, they only spent the night together on special occasions, like tonight.

And she intended to make it count.

The lock clicked and Sean's head poked through the opening. Instead of inviting her in, he grinned at her, and she instantly grew suspicious. "Okay, what are you hiding?"

His look turned to one of mock innocence. "Who says I'm hiding anything?"

She poked his nose with her forefinger. "I know you, Sean Fisher, and you're hiding something. If you don't let me in, I'll just find somewhere else to sleep tonight and you'll miss out on my two Christmas presents for you."

"Presents?"

She couldn't help but smile as his cougar's curiosity shined out of his eyes. "Yep, both are one of a kind and are Lauren Spencer originals."

He started to open the door but then stopped as he shook his head. "No, I want to give you my surprise first since it's all set up. The instant you come inside, the surprise will be ruined. Close your eyes and I'll guide you. Then you can give me yours afterward."

Her heart skipped a few beats. She teased Sean for loving surprises, but she was no different.

Still, she knew her cougar-shifter well enough to clarify a few things. "This surprise doesn't involve a white coat, handcuffs, and a vibrator does it?"

Laughing, he held out a hand to her. "No, not this time. Now, give me your hand, baby. It's killing me to have you here and not show you my surprise."

Placing her hand in his, she grinned. "Well, someone has to keep your silly-ass antics in check."

Sean squeezed her hand and his touch sent a little thrill through her body. His hands were large and warm, and could be very naughty when the man put his mind to it.

Just last night, those fingers had made her come twice before he'd even thrust his cock inside her.

A whistle shattered her memory of last night's steamy sex. The instant she met his gaze again, Sean's eyes flashed cougar blue. His voice was low and husky when he said, "Whatever you're thinking about, stop it. If you become any wetter, I won't be able to focus long enough to do this properly."

Of course. She should know by now that Sean could scent when she was aroused. Although, she wasn't quite sure she'd call it a drawback...

She banished the images of Sean and his thick, naughty fingers and closed her eyes. "Okay, I'm ready. The sooner you give me my surprise, the sooner I can give you yours."

She heard a grunt, and then felt Sean tug her forward as he placed a hand on her lower back. After taking a few awkward steps, Sean moved his hand from her back to her neck and squeezed lightly. "Open your eyes, Lauren."

As soon as she opened her eyes, Lauren gasped. Sean's entire apartment was decked out for Christmas.

On the far side of the room, the lopsided Christmas tree was adorable, as was the haphazard way he'd hung the ornaments and the garland. Lights lined the ceiling, flashing in some kind of pattern that sparkled off the glass snowflakes hanging nearby. There were even two giant, red stockings laying on the coffee table next to a stuffed Christmas bear. The plate of slightly burnt cookies in the shape of reindeers made her heart squeeze; Sean didn't cook often, but he'd attempted to make cookies for her.

Sean's voice filled her ears. "Well? How did I do?"

Turning back toward him, she said, "Oh, Sean. It's amazing."

Happiness flashed in his eyes and she couldn't resist putting her arms up to rest on either side of his neck. His arms instantly went around her waist, and his warmth and male scent surrounded her in that sense of comfort, safety, and love she always felt when her cougar held her close.

There was also no denying his thick, hard cock against her stomach. Yet more wetness rushed between her legs and Sean's nostrils flared as he said, "Lauren, I'm tempted to rip off your clothes right now."

Since he could extend his claws while in human form, she knew he wasn't bluffing.

As she caressed the skin at the back of his neck with one of her thumbs, she whispered, "Not before I give you one of my presents."

"Fuck your present. You're turned on and I need to take care of you."

That was a bonus she'd learned about shifters—they usually made sure their females orgasmed first.

"No." She stepped back and he let his arms fall with a growl. She smiled at the mix of understanding and possessiveness. "Stop pouting. I think you'll like what I have for you."

"Then hurry up. I want to fuck you at least three times before dinner."

Heat flashed through her body and her nipples hardened at the image of Sean taking her against the wall, then over the table, and maybe in the shower. Her man always surprised her, and she loved him for it.

But tonight, it was her turn to surprise him.

She cleared her throat. "Wait here." She took two steps and then added, "And no peeking."

Crossing his arms over his broad, muscled chest, Sean grunted. "You have five minutes before I come find you."

She tried to frown but failed. "Believe me, it'll be worth it."

Sean's expression softened. "Baby, you're always worth it."

Her throat tightened with emotion. Rather than have her voice crack, she nodded, picked up the bag she'd brought with her, and rushed into the bathroom to change.

==================

Cougar's First Christmas
Available Now

For exclusive content and updates, sign up for my newsletter at:
http://www.jessiedonovan.com

SACRIFICED TO THE DRAGON

In exchange for a vial of dragon's blood to save her brother's life, Melanie Hall offers herself up as a sacrifice to one of the British dragon-shifter clans. Being a sacrifice means signing a contract to live with the dragon-shifters for six months to try to conceive a child. Her assigned dragonman, however, is anything but easy. He's tall, broody, and alpha to the core. There's only one problem—he hates humans.

Due to human dragon hunters killing his mother, Tristan MacLeod despises humans. Unfortunately, his clan is in desperate need of offspring to repopulate their numbers and it's his turn to service a human female. Despite his plans to have sex with her and walk away, his inner dragon has other ideas. The curvy human female tempts his inner beast like no other.

==================

Sacrificed to the Dragon
Paperback Now Available

BLAZE OF SECRETS
(AMT #1)

Kiarra Melini overhears the dangerous secrets of her blood and decides that if *Feiru* elemental magic is to survive, she needs to die. However, before she can finish the deed, a strange yet determined man shows up in her cell, throws her over his shoulder, and carries her right out of the prison for elemental magic users.

Jaxton Ward is ordered by his superiors to train the stubborn elemental fire user he rescued. There's only one problem—she claims her magic is gone and he has no idea how to train a woman who spent the last fifteen years inside a prison cell. He's determined to keep his relationship professional, but as the danger amps up and they're forced to go on the run, he starts to fall for the newly confident woman who ignites his temper like no other.

Kiarra's final secret is the key to them staying alive, but can they outrun the prison enforcers long enough for her to embrace her unique magical talents and finally learn to love again?

===================

Blaze of Secrets

Paperback Now Available

Author's Note

First off, while I always try my best to get my facts right in my stories, it is highly probable that some of my techie stuff is wrong. If that is the case, then I claim author's artistic license!

With that out of the way, I wanted to thank a few people:

—Thank you to Virginia, Becky, and all the ladies at Hot Tree Editing. I appreciate all of your help in making my story shine. :)

—A huge, huge thank you to my cover designer, Clarissa Yeo of Yocla Designs. She makes the most amazing covers. Not only that, she doesn't so much as bat an eye when I ask for a Native American/American Indian heroine on the cover (like this one). Thanks Clarissa!

—Another shout out to The Wolf Pack. You all are amazing in your support and constant stream of man candy. Thank you!

—And finally, a huge thank you to my beta reader, Donna H., for her suggestions.

And most of all, I want to thank you, the reader. I'm grateful for all my readers and fans, and I hope you join me over on my Facebook Author Page (facebook.com/JessieDonovanAuthor) to have some fun or just to drop me a line. I always respond!

Now, I'm off to write some more books…

ABOUT THE AUTHOR

Jessie Donovan wrote her first story at age five, and after discovering *The Dragonriders of Pern* series by Anne McCaffrey in junior high, she realized people actually wanted to read stories like those floating around inside her head. From there on out, she was determined to tap into her over-active imagination and write a book someday.

After living abroad for five years and earning degrees in Japanese, Anthropology, and Secondary Education, she buckled down and finally wrote her first full-length book. While that story will never see the light of day, it laid the world-building groundwork of what would become her debut paranormal romance, *Blaze of Secrets*. In October 2014, she became a USA Today Bestselling author.

Jessie loves to interact with readers, and when not traipsing around some foreign country on a shoestring, can often be found on Facebook and Twitter. Check out her pages below:

http://www.facebook.com/JessieDonovanAuthor
http://www.twitter.com/jessiedauthor

And don't forget to sign-up for her newsletter to receive sneak peeks and inside information. You can sign-up on her website:

http:///www.jessiedonovan.com

Made in the USA
Las Vegas, NV
10 December 2021

36732076R00132